D0264339

'Before picking up a Julie Burchill book you can be sure of two things. Firstly, the writing will fizz, crackle and zing off the page with the style and panache that are truly, unruly Julie. Forget Kathy Lette or Helen Fielding – this woman writes the backside off her contemporaries . . . Secondly, you feel quite safe in the knowledge that the central character – here Nicole Miller, a thirtysomething, hard-drinking illustrator in London – is pretty much Ms Burchill herself' *Mirror*

'Dazzling passages light up the book . . . Baleful, angry, with a manic energy, this is the page-turner . . . that makes you laugh' *Independent*

'As ever, you can't fault her writing: it gambols and skips along . . . You'll have as much fun reading it as Burchill did writing it' *Heat*

'We should love Burchill for being the anti-Bridget Jones. This is – shock, horror – a popular woman's novel without calorie counts or an Ally McBeal-style flake as the so-called heroine. Put it this way. Who would you rather read about: sappy Bridget, whose self-esteem depends on her bloke and bathroom scales? Or manic Nicole, who takes revenge on her husband by serving up her grandma's false teeth when his trendy mates come to dinner? My vote goes to the dentures' *Manchester Evening News*

'Just occasionally Julie Burchill allows Nicole to make sweeping judgements in the manner of that brilliant and idiosyncratic journalist Julie Burchill; but what is persuasive about Nicole's character is the way in which she is aggressively confident and sadly vulnerable by turns . . . [I] enjoyed *Married Alive*' Paul Bailey, *Daily Telegraph*

By the same author

Ambition
No Exit
Love It or Shove It
Damaged Gods
Sex and Sensibility
Girls on Film
I Knew I Was Right
Diana

Born in Bristol in 1959, Julie Burchill is known for her controversial and acerbic style of journalism. At seventeen she went to work for the *New Musical Express*, at nineteen *The Face*, at twenty-four the *Sunday Times*. She has written for many magazines and national newspapers and is the author of eight previous books, including her autobiography, *I Knew I Was Right*, and her biography of Diana, Princess of Wales, which was published in 1998 to universal acclaim.

Married Alive

Julie **Burchill**

691825
MORAY COUNCIL
DEPARTMENT OF TECHNICAL
& LEISURE SERVICES
F

An Orion Paperback
First published in Great Britain by Orion in 1999
This paperback edition published in 1999 by Orion Books Ltd,
Orion House, 5 Upper St Martin's Lane, London WC2H 9EA

Copyright © 1999 Julie Burchill

The right of Julie Burchill to be identified as the author of this work has been asserted by her in accordance with the Copyright, Designs and Patents Act 1988.

All rights reserved. No part of this publication may be reproduced, stored in a retrieval system, or transmitted, in any form or by any means, electronic, mechanical, photocopying, recording or otherwise, without the prior permission of the copyright owner.

The characters and events in this book are fictitious. Any similarity to real persons, living or dead, is coincidental.

A CIP catalogue record for this book is available from the British Library.

ISBN: 0 75282 682 4

Printed and bound in Great Britain by
Clays Ltd, St Ives plc

For Daniel

Chapter **One**

I woke up around midday, sick as the proverbial. And, of course, I started complaining straight away.

'Why me, God?' (obvious), 'Never again!' (physically possible, but with my track record highly unlikely) – and then, of course, I wanted my mother. It's sad, isn't it? A tragic farce. Pathetic. And *that's* utilising English understatement to the max.

I made a dash for the bathroom. This is the only time I ever run since I left school – when I'm about to throw. (This tells you something about my life, I think. Just a teeny something.) So I'm holding on to the porcelain, as though I'm praying, or as if I've heard that Daniel Day-Lewis once sat there, I'm throwing up and thinking about my mother – and these really aren't such good things to do at any time, like singly, are they? Let alone both at once.

I was thinking – I've started so I'll finish – of how my mother always wrote that I'd had a 'bilious attack' on Tuesday afternoons, when I was trying to get off Double Games. I'd have had to pretend to vomit, first, of course; you can try this at home, and whatever you do don't ask a grown-up first. My best ruse was to cook up a Bird's Eye boil-in-the-bag meal for one – Beef Stew & Dumplings was pretty cool, and being a very *profound* brown really looked like serious sick – wolf most of it then smear a few tablespoons round the toilet bowl. As soon as I heard my mum's key in the door, I'd stagger down the stairs all bleary and teary, gesturing grimly towards the upper storey of our suburban semi as though I had one of my uncles, greased and naked, kneeling on my virginal bed.

'Don't go up there!' I'd croak. 'I haven't had time to –'

Natch, she'd run upstairs sweet as a nut, and discover the steamy mess. I'd get my sick note; if she was feeling especially generous, I'd get the day off. Fantastic! I could then sit around all afternoon slugging Corona, watching *Houseparty* on the tube and checking out the beautiful view in the mirror.

You'd have thought she'd have cocoa'd earlier that I *always* brought up Beef Stew & Dumplings, wouldn't you, though? Be fair. And simply told me to lay off it for the duration and get with the boil-in-the-bag Cod in Parsley Sauce for a while. Brain food. But she wasn't exactly Einstein, my mum, or even Epstein. Good gams, though – and legs are hereditary, apparently. 'Legs are a girl's best friend,' Matt's always saying – I mean, *always*. 'But even best friends have to part sometime!' What a wit, eh? Reader – I laughed at his jokes.

I staggered back to bed and looked gingerly around the loft – not all at once, but bit by bit, like an ugly girl looking in the mirror. It was a sight for eyes so sore they'd need a bucketful of Murine to put them right, all right – there are few minor things more depressing,

I feel, than the debris of hedonism. And I could see it all so clearly, amazingly enough, as it had been the night before – in the wee small hours, just a while ago.

'Why do they call them the wee small hours?' Zoë asked, pointing at me with a bottle of Bolly.

'Um . . .'

'Because by that time you've drunk so much that you have to take a leak every five minutes!'

We literally fell about. Yes, reader, it was that kind of evening.

The kind of evening that the word 'cocooning' was invented for, the kind of evening which makes you wonder hard why anyone ever goes out unless it's to score a pint of drugs. Absolut on ice, Ella on the stereo and Zoë on my face – just kidding, heh, heh! Respectable married woman, me. I could see the loft, which looked quite a lot like Ice Station Zebra Crossing during the day, all dark and cave-like – won't say 'womb-like', whoah, not me, not now I'm being analysed with the best, or at least the rest of them.

'I'm being analysed,' I told my mother.

'Is that anything like colonic irrigation, like what the princess had?' she goes, all ears, no brain.

I could see it all cosy with low lights and redwood floors and the kitsch artificial fire which my friends all laughed at but held out their hands to anyway, flickering licks of love all over Zoë and Lucy and Emma and me. Zoë, Lucy and fucking Emma, I ask you! – three little maids from public school! This too, to me, says something about my life: when I was at school, in my natural environment, shall we say, all my friends were called Susan and Julie. I mean *all*. They had to identify themselves like rappers would do later – Julie B, Susan T. Dead cool. But now, I open my phone book and I'm *assaulted* by nancy gangs of Cressidas and Carolines and Clemencies, and of course my nearest and dearest, my effing Zoës and Lucys and Emmas.

'It's Emma – Emma Young,' one of them will go on the phone.

'Yes, yes,' I'll snap nastily. 'How many fucking Emmas do you think I know?'

She's a good girl, this one, so she doesn't answer, but I can tell what she's thinking. She's thinking, Oh dear; Nicole's lost her roots. What she doesn't know is that Nicole's lost her ruddy A, too. I was born Nicola Sharp, but by art school I thought it was common; too late I caught on that an English working-class name is a whole lot cooler than a French tart's name, which can never be cool though it can be camp. But by then, as I said, it seemed too late. ('Too late'; are they the worst words in the world, or what? Even worse than 'I can't do the zip up'?) I got spliced, God help me; Nicola Sharp had become Nicole Miller. I was shafted, on my own sensibility.

I got out of bed and had a closer shufti. There was stuff all over the floor. You know – stuff. The sort of thing of which your mother would say, 'What's this?', holding it between her thumb and forefinger, glaring at you. Rolled-up banknotes. Cigarette filters, but no cigarettes. Paperback books with bits torn off. Personally, I don't like to think about how much money's worth of stuff we'd got through last night between the four of us. I'll tell you the problem with drugs; whereas most things are either the problem or the solution, drugs are the problem *and* the solution. Believe it.

I screwed up my courage and looked in the Bag. God. Who visited here and took home a souvenir while I was asleep? The Drug Fairy? Is she related to the Tooth Fairy, by any chance? Yes, that's it: the Tooth Fairy gets the teeth, the Drug Fairy gets the drugs. The Tooth Fairy leaves you money, the Drug Fairy bankrupts you. Well, I know which gig *I* want when I grow up.

I wanted to clear up – really I did, Your Honour – but I didn't have the stomach for it. (I'd left it in the toilet bowl, still waiting for Daniel Day-Lewis to revisit the scene of the crime, remember.) I just went back to bed, lying there looking at it all – My Sin, like that old scent bottle, before scents were called things like Slag and Skag – and trying to put together the night before. It was like trying to put together that horrible Escher jigsaw my mother bought me to torment me with when I was off school with hayfever one year for six weeks. Honestly, my eyes were out on stalks – literally – and I'm trying to piece together all these guys going up staircases that lead nowhere and all look the same. No wonder I had a sense of *déjà-vu* the first time I went to the National Theatre. Or that could have been because I was with Matthew, yippee-skippy, and all his gags were so fucking old.

Anyway, I wouldn't have sworn on the Bible, or even the latest *Details*, but I believe things turned out this way: Lucy turned up at eight, straight from work, bringing Zoë and three bottles of Moët. We sat on the floor and played moaning records by complicated American women. I'll tell you when you know you're drunk, girls: you put on Janis Ian singing 'At Seventeen' and you say to your friends, completely seriously:

'It's you – it's me – it's all of us!' Zoë said she was through with men. She said this for two and a half hours, if you please. Then, get this, then her mobile rings; it was her ex, with sex on his pecs in some dismal Tex-Mex. Would you believe, she was off like a shot! Even left her line! She was like the Flash: just a blur of light, and then nothing.

I look at Lucy, pointing and gaping. I'm a sculpture called 'Women Are Their Own Worst Enemies'. 'Did you see that? Or am I going mad?'

Lucy nods. 'You are going mad, but I did see it.' Her voice is like being shot up with Pimms fruit cup; those cucumber slices are a bastard on your arteries. Then she smiles, all bittersweet like. Bittersweet, there's a phoney word; just means lousy, with gilded knobs on. 'Have *you* seen *him*?'

'I have had that pleasure, I believe. Though not horizontally, unlike most of Zoë's cronies.'

'Well, come on. He looks a lot like Robert Newman. You can't really blame her.'

'Well, isn't that coochie,' I say, dead surly. 'Because *she* looks a lot like David Baddiel.' This was unfair; she doesn't really. Not in an artificial light. If it's peach. And twenty-watt.

The buzzer went and it was Emma. 'Emma Crewe,' this one ventures hopefully. I *hate* that.

'I know,' I snapped. 'How many fucking Emmas do you think I know?'

Now this one isn't as sweet, or as smart, as the other one, Emma Young. Nor is she, we may safely say, as sensitive. So she stands there in the street, searching her tiny loose-leafed personal organiser of a mind for an answer as the pages blow away unnoticed down the dark *film noir* street. 'Well, there's Emma Young, Emma Hope, Emma Forrest, Emma Ballantine, Emma with the tattoo, no, that's Gemma –'

'Oh for God's sake!' I buzzed her in and looked at Lucy. I wished I looked *like* Lucy. She sat there doing her Wistfully Luminous routine by the fire, looking like an Alice in Wonderland who'd married Lewis Carroll and woken up with the Jabberwocky, all blonde and English. It's funny about these girls, these girls who went to St Mary's, Calne, and stuff: they make you feel like a foreigner, even if you don't have a drop of Dago blood.

'What's up, sugar-shovel?' I asked.

She shook her head; her slide fell out. Days after Lucy's been and gone I find all this stuff she puts on and in her hair. Slides. Snoods. Combs. Hairbands. All that weird stuff. It *is* weird, putting stuff in your hair. (Unless it comes out of a tube.) Tribal. The ancient tribe of the happy-sad very-English upper-class almost-beautiful nearly-smart girl. 'Oh, I . . . oh. It's just William.'

I nodded grimly. Just William. That's what we call him, Zoë and Emma and me. Because it makes sense. A certain sort of man starts out as a sly, lying, cheating schoolboy, a Just William, to whom women above all are the enemy, and they end up being the Just William that's ruining a woman's one and only life with their sly lies that they've been told are so cute. You see, this one's trouble, this Lucy, is that it's in love with a married man. Excuse me – did I say 'man'? No – I won't call it a 'man'. To me, a 'man' who cheats on his wife isn't a man at all – he's a pig, or a rat, or something else the Chinese have years for. Oooo!

you're going by now; oooo! She sounds bitter! She's obviously suffered at the hands of a married man! Well, you're damn right I have – and he's called *my husband*.

Well, I thought that might shut you up! Don't mess with the bull – you'll get the horns! Anyway, up comes Emma, tight as a tourniquet. She's hoovered up half of West Wonderland tonight, and she's not in a mind to stop till she drops. So one thing leads to another – out come the Doors CDs – and it seems a bit naff to think about tomorrow when Lucy's down, Emma's up and Jim's urging us to break on through to the other side (of what? I never dared ask) so, before you know it, that nice little stash I've been keeping *solely* for working purposes, and *only* gave Zoë and Lucy a teensy-weensy sniff of, comes *right* out, lines up and marches off to meet its maker.

We had a brilliant time – I remember *that* much. You do, don't you? When the blow is flowing and the drink is sinking, there's no one in the world that's not a fascinating bastard from Bacchanalia. Even your old friend you've had this conversation with one thousand times before; it's all new, all too tender to touch. And in the morning, of course, those very same fascinating bastards from Bacchanalia have cleared you out! Well, you think, *next* time I'll know the signs: don't talk to fascinating bastards from Bacchanalia! But the trick is this: *fascinating bastards always come disguised as your dull old friends!*

That is why cocaine is, in its way, such a *fairy-tale* drug. It's not a downer like smack. It's not a nuisance like speed. It's pixie dust: we can fly, we can fly, we can fly, and we can make people follow us! We can get the freak out of Hamlyn, our posse prancing at our heels, and waltz right in – plus twenty – to Never-Never Land. Ha! Bloody irony, don't you just love it? Because Never-Never Land is right: once you get the taste for cocaine, you'd better be a dentist or you'll never-never be in the black again. Trust me, I'm a modern.

I looked around, dead furtive, like I was being closely observed with a secret camera; I needed *one more line*. Then I could clean up. Then I could paint my masterpiece, or at least my toenails. Then, after a light luncheon in which all the nutritious food groups were modestly represented, I could bring about world peace.

Except . . . once you've *had* that line, you don't feel the *need* to do any of the above. Why, they seem almost . . . *in bad taste*. Pushing it. What you *really* want to do, what you know *in your bones* you should do, is put on *The Lexicon of Love*, groove around with your make-up bag for a spell and talk for hours on the phone with your friends – because if we are not friends to our friends, then how can we be friends to the world? – about whether FABs were better than LUVs, whatever happened to Ayesha Brough and Aztec bars and whether or not you should become a Catholic ('because it's the only thing I haven't done' – cheesy snicker, which actually sounds like some sort of new confectionery).

Yeah, don't talk to *me* about the morning after, brother. The hair of the black dog that bit you. I've *been* there. Been there so often I've got a season ticket. Got my own seat on the train – the other ravers save it for me if I'm late. Been there so often the train won't go without me. Nothing left to burn. Stick *that* in your pipe.

Do you know what ghost-busting is? It's when, like, against all evidence, you just *know* you've got *one more gram* hidden away somewhere. It's just a really dumb thing that people do when their recreational drug use gets out of control. When it's getting to be a Habit. I hate people who are out of control like that – it's *so* Eighties. Well, anyway, I'd just located Matthew's chisel, pliers and electric drill and was all set to get to work on that loose board by the bathroom door when the phone rang.

And of course it was That Voice. The one I longed for, sighed for, dreaded every time the phone rang. It was a West Country voice, that uniquely vulnerable and unmodernised voice, a voice which seemed to simply yell out, however hushed: 'Hello, all you carpetbaggers and conmen out there! Why don't you come round and fleece me blind one day? Just before lunch is best, because I'm always out at the shops then – you can be in and out in ten minutes without ever having to suffer the embarrassment of looking me in the eye. Tell you what – I'll leave the key under the mat! Can't say fairer than that, now, can I?'

None of the spivviness of the South or the chippiness of the North, that voice; the voice I'd lost, like having dermabrasion, so something better could be born. And so now I was another thirtyish 'girl' from Nowhere, resident in London but not really belonging to it and well past an age when I seriously believed it could ever belong to me; with a voice, and the rest of it, from which all thoughts of social class or regional distinction – and to me, being a working-class girl from the

West Country *is* actually a distinction, somehow; not just a difference – had been blanched until I was now just a bad, blurred xerox of the person I used to be. I was healthy and affluent and I enjoyed my work – and, quite frankly, there were now at least three days in every month when I woke up and wished I was dead. And they *weren't* just before my period, either, for the information of all you tittering guys out there, thank you. And it wasn't anything to do with needing a good seeing-to or feminism or having a job or not having children because people, not just women, have been experiencing this since the first caveperson woke up one morning, went to wash his/her face in the clear crystal stream and then moaned: 'Oh fuck, not *you* again.' It's a condition, potentially life-threatening, called human – and there's not a damn thing you can do about it.

Come on, Nicola, cheer us all up! Anyway, the phone – it was my mother, Teresa. You call her Terry, and she'll call you an ambulance. This is one mean lady, see. This is the woman who almost made me come from the lower middle class, and you don't get a lot meaner than that. But I saw to her. Her and her crinoline ladies on the toilet rolls. I know this seems a bit rich now, considering I've done the rough equivalent of it to my voice. But I wasn't going to have *my* brilliant start in life, my working-class blood royal called into question by no crinoline lady on no roll of Andrex. No way!

My mother didn't sound so cocky now, though, bless her American Tan nylon tights, as she struggled manfully with my answering machine. You'd think it was a disembodied voice from the grave the way she was carrying on, stuttering and stammering like a speedfreak on *Mastermind*. Though the joke is that if it *had* been a disembodied voice from the grave she'd probably have been quite at home with it, having spent a goodly part of her youth messing around with Ouija boards and having her palm read, as you do. But an answering machine was way beyond her.

'Nicola?' Her voice wobbled, like a bicycle. 'Do I speak now, Tom?' That was my dad, who I definitely should have married, looking back. 'Nicola, it's Mummer. I mean your mother. Mum. Teresa Sharp.' She stopped, having transmitted this earth-moving message, well pleased with herself.

I looked around the room, dead guilty. I pulled at my T-shirt, trying to get it down over my thighs; fat chance, seeing as how it wasn't a barrage balloon. I'd noticed this thing about my thighs recently – that they always went to bed ten minutes after I did. Like we were at boarding school and they were in a higher form or something. Then I rushed blindly at the beached pleasure zone, scattering roaches and rolled-up banknotes as I ran, in some strange parody of housewifery.

The rolled-up banknote is a big thing with me; last time I saw my dad – he and Mum were up for the wedding – I inadvertently left a rolled-up fiver on the restaurant table to tip a waitress with. My dad picked it up and looked through it, squinting: ' "I see," said Nelson – lookin' through 'is telescope with 'is blind eye!'

Him and me and Matt cracked up; the Basque waitress (country of origin, not mode of dress, worst luck) smiled as though her feet were killing her. But my mother, old Mother Teresa over there, gave me what can only be described as a Look. She'd probably seen it on *The Bill*, banknotes like that. Once, when I was a teenager, she asked me if I was taking L.S. Speed. At school, in the West Country, in the Seventies, when the only pop group we'd produced was the Wurzels! What a laugh! If I took three Junior Disprin I thought I was living it up! But my mother ran a tight ship; that she habitually got half-cut on advocaat and lemonade ('snowball' is, I believe; the 'correct' name for this beverage) every Saturday night and treated my father and me to chronic renditions of 'The Boers Have Got My Daddy' and 'My Canary's Got Circles Under His Eyes' was neither here nor there, apparently.

'It's about Gran,' she said.

I stopped, frozen like a tooth under cocaine, which was a bit appropriate actually as I'd found a stray smidgin of the stuff and was rubbing it into my gums. This American pop star taught me to do this when I was seventeen; it doesn't do Sam Hill, but what the heck, it *looks* good.

My throat closed up, like when some clever dick tries to make you do irrigation or irrumation or whatever it's called, and I knew I was going to cry and cry and probably never stop crying. This was it, this was the big one. My gran was dead.

I sleepwalked over to the answering machine and looked at it, so black and sleek and smug and . . . machiney, I suppose. My mother's voice droned on; she seemed none too upset.

'Yesss . . . iss about Gran. Iss for the best, really.' Heartless bitch; I never really liked her. All those Mother's Day cards: complete payola. Not that she deserved them. The first one I ever made for her, at school, I spelt it HAPPY MOTORING DAY. I was only six, for Pete's sake! She took one look at it, said, 'I can't drive' and chucked it in the bin! 'But I thought I should tell you. She's going this Sunday . . .'

What was this, some kind of euthanasia kick? I pictured my mother's *Daily Mirror* Animal Friends calendar with a neat red ring around the coming Sunday: THREE P.M. (AFTER EASTENDERS): KILL GRAN. I snatched up the phone.

'Hello, hello, Mum? What *is* this?'

'Oh – Nicola.' She sounded so sheepish I could have made a polo-neck sweater out of her. 'I thought you'd want to know . . .'

'Damn right I want to know! Do you realise what you're doing, woman? You're transgressing against every moral code ever known to man! The Judaic . . . and the Mosaic . . . and stuff . . .'

'What mosaics?' The murderous witch actually had the nerve to sound indignant. 'She's not being sent to ruddy Australia, you know!'

'Mother. It's a bit further than that, actually, isn't it?'

'No iss not. Iss the other side of Chipping Sodbury.'

I sort of cottoned on to something here. You know the expression 'It's the drink talking'? Well, in this case it was the coke listening. I'd jumped to quite a drastic conclusion, to say the least. But you see, this little exchange does tell you something, even if I was wrong. It tells you that my mother's a bit of a cold fish when she's not running on pure alcohol, and that there's no telling what she'd do after a few snowballs if someone

– or their incontinence problem – stood between her and that new three-piece suite.

'*What's* on the other side of Chipping Sodbury?' I said slowly.

'The Home,' she said, bold as Brasso.

'The Huh –' I couldn't even say it – 'What d'you mean, the Huh – Huh? She's got a bloody home!'

'She *hasn't* got a home.' Madam was really getting into her stride now. 'She's got a *flat*. A flat whose front door, you might know if you ever honoured us with your presence, she leaves unlocked all day and all evening long. She locks it just before she goes to bed – eleven o'clock at night! In the roughest part of Bristol, too – 'cept for St Paul's,' she added hurriedly. That's the Negro quarter of Bristol's fair city, fact fans. Racist cow. 'As though she was still living in Victory Street! As though she still knows her neighbours and there wasn't gangs of them mugger buggers running round them flats that would kill you for the lint on your jumper!' She was really getting into her stride now, oh yes! 'Thass not a home, Nicola – thass a time bomb waiting to go like a lamb to the slaughter.' My mother, you might have noticed, believes that metaphors are there purely to be picked and mixed like cheap sweeties at Woolworth, really she does.

'So, basically what you're saying, and please correct me if I'm wrong, is that you're having her put away. Gran.'

'Not *away*, Nicola,' merciful old Mother Teresa gets in quickly. I could tell I'd hit home there, or even hit *the* Home, or whatever. 'Ajar,' she added callously.

'Away. Ajar. On one side of your plate for the bin men to cart away. I don't care what the frig –'

'Ooo! Language!'

'Mother, I didn't say "fuck", I said "frig", OK? I don't care what the frig you call it, anyway! For God's sake, woman –'

'Ohhh! "Woman", is it, now?'

'– this is your own flesh and blood we're talking about!'

'Your father's, actually, Nicola!'

Get her – Dorothy Parker after swallowing Oscar Wilde whole. 'Whatever,' I snapped. 'It's immaterial. You *can't* put her away into one of those places, you just can't. She'll become a, a . . . a *vegetable.*'

It's strange, isn't it, how vegetables have become both saint and sinner in this our modern world? When the nutritionists are on the warpath, it's 'Eat more vegetables and you'll live to be a hundred!' Yet when you've gone ahead and lived to be a hundred, and we want to describe the worst possible state a crumbly of that grand old age can get themselves into, we say they're 'a vegetable'! Talk about 'You are what you eat.' Wouldn't that be a great slogan for greengrocers? EAT MORE VEGETABLES – AND BECOME ONE!

Well, great minds think alike, *not*, because then my mother goes all quiet and says in what she amazingly imagines to be a 'wry' voice: 'Nicola, in eighty-five years your grandmother has never even *eaten* a vegetable unless it came out of a chip pan, so far as I know. She certainly isn't going to turn into one at this late stage. She's got a will of iron and a constitution of brainless steel.' She stopped, then started. 'I meant *stainless* steel. Slip of the tongue.'

Slip of the knife, more like. A stainless-steel bread-knife, right through the Zimmer frame. But I decide to be real cool about it. 'That's OK, Mum,' I breeze, all Zen-calm to Teresa's bilious Diacalm. 'I'm not mad at you, honest; I'm just sad *for* you. None of this is your fault; it's just a symptom of the crazy way we live now in the West.'

Teresa thought about this. When she spoke, her voice was soft and curious, almost sweet. Like a child's. 'What, the way we live in Bristol?'

'No,' I hissed. 'I wasn't *talking* about the west of England. I meant *Europe*.' I thought about this. 'Except Italy. And Spain, I guess. Portugal, too, perhaps. I meant northern Europe and North America – and Australia, I suppose.'

She was interested now, in her own pin-headed sort of way. 'Not New Zealand, though?'

'Yes!' I yelled. 'And in bloody New Zealand too! Tasmania, you name it. God!' I pulled myself up quick. 'Sorry, Mum, I'm getting a bit tense. I've got to chill out this end.' I got with the abbreviated neck massage and a little light chanting. I wouldn't call myself a Buddhist, strictly speaking – never been much of a Joiner – but I definitely believe in a Force.

'Nicola?' There was panic in my mother's voice. Good. 'What's going on? Who's making that noise? Who have you got there?'

'The Dalai Lama and Richard Gere – what's it sound like?' Here I was, completely losing it. 'Mother. Please forgive me. I just –'

'You only ever call me Mother when you think I've done something wrong.'

'You haven't done anything wrong. *Mum*,' I soothed. 'Not *as such*. It's just the way we're used to behaving in the West now – not especially Bristol. If something doesn't fit into our nice selfish scheme of things, why, we just bin it and do a runner.'

'What, like you did when you went off to London, you mean?'

Mothers – who'd have 'em? '*No*, Mother – that was *not* a selfish whim on my part we're talking about there. That was a matter of life and death and sanity. I had a place at St Martin's, in case you'd forgotten.'

Dead surly: 'We got an art school here.'

'And for those unfortunate souls whose life's ambition is to lay out the *Bristol Evening Post*, I'm sure it's a hoot. I personally would rather drink my own methylated spirits *after* I've cleaned my brushes in it, but it takes all sorts to make a bag of liquorice. Anyway, that's beside the point.'

'Well, what is the point then? Look lively, iss my Meals on Wheels day down 'ere. My old ladies are waiting for me.'

Did you hear that? Ego-crazed, self-centred cow! 'My' old ladies, if you please – as though they weren't valid, autonomous people in their own right! I sighed quite loudly, but non-judgementally, sort of like a saint. 'The point *is*, Mother, if you can spare a minute for your own daughter between orgies of self-servingness –'

'Iss not self-service. I serve 'em meself.'

'– the point *is*, as I was saying, that in other cultures less materialistic and neurotic than our own, people *treasure* the old – elderly – mature, I mean. They *learn* from them.'

'No they don't,' my mother said smugly. 'They send them out begging in the street.'

I laughed at her, quite good-naturedly considering

the outrageous provocation being offered. 'Really, Mother! Where did you pick up *that* little gem? The *National Front News*?'

'No, from Mrs Noorani. One of my old ladies. Lovely woman, she is – came from Pakistan years ago. Told me that not a day passes when she doesn't get down on her knees and thank some god or other that she was allowed to come here. Anyway, she *used* to get down on her knees – until her arthritis got what it came for. 'Er 'ands,' my mother deliberated with a relish I'm sure she didn't display for the Meals on Wheels themselves, 'are like claws. *Claws*.'

Well, it had taken her all of six minutes but my mother was now primed and ready to launch into her virtuoso performance. Tonight and every night, ladies and gentlemen: Teresa Sharp on illness, infirmity and that finale of finales, D.E.A.T.H.! Like most working-class women between the ages of nineteen and ninety-one, Mrs Sharp literally lives for her subject and has really done her homework.

I'm sure somewhere there must be some sort of Disease Fantasy League all these broads are plugged into, like the Internet: fifty points for a stroke, seventy-five for your major cancers, a hundred for a double amputation. I know we all have to get our kicks somehow, as the current state of my happy home bears mute witness to. But this morbid fascination with pain and torment is one facet of my blue-collar blood-royal background I have never been able to get with. The ordinary state of marriage should be enough to satisfy such cravings comfortably.

So I tackled her fast: 'Mum, stop this! We're not talking about your Mrs Noorani and her squalid rheumatics; we're talking about *my grandmother*! Don't you have *any* feelings of responsibility towards your own kith and kin? Like, um . . .' I knew what I meant, but I didn't have the words, you know?

Teresa said: 'What, like in the Falklands?'

'No!' My patience was running out now. 'Like history! Continuity! Like *roots*.'

'The day you left Bristol you said only trees had roots.' She sounded mutinous now. And by the way, I *never* said that.

'I didn't say that. Or if I did, I said it in the Seventies. Or the Eighties. We're nicer now.' I flipped the Idea over one more time in my mind, like a pancake bitter with lemon, and went for it. 'Listen – I'm coming to get her. Tell Gran that – that Nic-Nic's coming to rescue her. From you fair-weather . . . biological descendants and in-laws alike. And I don't need anyone's help. Do you hear me? Anything needs to be done, I'll do it myself.' I stopped to have a think. 'Actually, could Dad pick me up from the station?'

Chapter **Two**

Apparently, some people – women, if you must (not me; married woman!) – well, we'll call her Zoë because that's her name – anyway, some people who are a bit *cynical* say that men talk to women so they'll sleep with them, while women sleep with men so they'll talk to them. This is a pretty depressing take on what ought to be one of nature's wonders – like dolphins – I'll grant you. But then, seeing as how dolphins themselves are well into troilism (three-in-a-seabed romps, if you will), ceaseless one-night stands (and you wondered why they were always smiling!) and for all I know selling their first-born to Jacques Cousteau, I suppose they're not much of a shining example. Quite frankly, what Flipper got up to between takes doesn't really bear thinking about: a dolphin's sex-drive and a star's pulling power.

Anyway; women want to talk and men want to rut. And at the bottom line, you can see this in the way men go to hookers (I hate that word, but what else is there? 'Whore' makes them sound like they're having multiple orgasms all over the place, 'sex worker' sounds so soulless and German, while 'tart' – well, in the West Country, old people call any beloved young woman a 'tart'. Their granddaughters and that) while women go to shrinks. They both cost. They both count the minutes and find that only fifty make an hour. And they both won't kiss you. Believe me, I've tried.

A word here. I don't want to seem utterly sad, like the high point of my day is rubbing perfumed magazine strips on my nipples or something. I did have people to talk to; I had Zoë, and Emma, and Lucy, and best of all the babe in the mirror.

But I wanted more, as you do: a *bona fide* trick cyclist.

Now I've heard horror stories from my nancy girlfriends about how shrinks of the male persuasion can cause more problems than they solve; they're not called 'therapists' (look how that word breaks up!) for nothing. Besides, they're all so ugly; definitely the type of guys who picked the big Montelimar in the chocolate box of life. If I'm trying to evict the essential me, I don't want to be worrying about some saddo's nasal hair.

That's why I've got my Dr Alibhai. Dr Alibhai not only has a great name, but she looks like the sort of amazing-looking Anglo brunettes who used to play Asian babes in Fifties films. I think her mother might be English, as they are. She makes brown not a boring colour: brown eyes, brown skin, brown voice. She must be about forty. But the best thing about her is, she doesn't give a damn about her job.

She pretends she's making notes, and really she's marking seed catalogues. I saw this once when there was a fire alarm (false).

Knowing she's not really listening, at least no more

than your second-best friend would, you feel free. This is an English thing.

'Are you sure you don't want to talk about your mother?'

I realised I was sucking my thumb and stopped. 'Who, me? No, not really. Thanks. Mothers are pretty much the same, aren't they? Scolding . . . holding you down . . .'

'Go on,' says Dr Alibhai, bending over her case notes. I can see blameless blooms just peeking over the top.

'Well, I suppose mothers are a necessary evil. Like . . . sugar. And you have to take your lumps.' Her lips moved as she saw a rose she liked the look of. I started to feel a little mutinous; I'm paying through the nose (literally, considering my habit) and she's tiptoeing through the tulips. I decided to come clean and let her get her hands dirty. 'No, I'd like to talk about my grandmother.'

'Shrubs,' Dr Alibhai muttered like a nutter. Then she looked up, dead guilty. 'Your grandmother?'

'Sorry. Does that cost twice as much?' A bit bratty here, I'm ashamed to say. I wouldn't have minded so much being second best to one perfect orchid; I'm an artist, aren't I? It was the shrubs that rubbed me up the wrong way.

Dr Alibhai realises here that she's gone a shrub too far, and to her credit she colours. A person of colour blushing isn't quite as hideous as a paleface doing the same, but it's just as much of a giveaway. She tucks her flora-porn under my notes and says very reasonably: 'Of course not, Nicola. Please go on.'

I lay back and closed my eyes. I would soon be

sunbathing, even there on that sticky couch, under a pointless ceiling. My memories were as warm and as dangerous and as irresistible as fireworks: light the touchpaper, and retreat. Never go back to the ones that lie dormant: they might go off in your face, blinding you to the rest of your life. But whoever resisted fireworks; especially the morning after, spent, useless? To me, then, they were at their most beautiful: the soaked, sapped cylinders with their primitive illustrations of what joys awaited us within the Roman Candle (this kills me about the English. Other countries, they think up the most grotesque, mother-mauling insults for minorities they feel threatened by. We call them after beautiful fireworks) and the Emerald Cascade. Are fireworks the only product which look *worse* on the package than they do in real life?

I remember going into our back garden the morning after, collecting the soggy shells while my mother watched irritably from the french windows. You should have seen her face as she barred my entry with my booty back into the house; you'd have thought she was La Pasionara turning back the Fascist hordes, at least. I wouldn't have minded if the house I'd grown up in had been some sort of stark, antiseptic, minimalist dream, but it was actually quite a tip: clean enough, and repapered with monotonous regularity (and always, it seemed, with the same anaemic wallpaper) but also a death trap and minefield sacrificed to the creature comforts of their mongrel dog, Benito. (Don't ask. I don't know, and I don't want to think about it.) Benito, unlike the human inhabitants of our home who lived under a reign of terror where crumbs were concerned, enjoyed the ancient bones of long-gone cattle and the dried ears of pigs, and left them scattered at intervals, like canapés or conversation pieces at a cocktail party, throughout the house. They were not nice to step on. The heartfelt cry of 'Jesus!' echoed through our home so endlessly and emphatically that the Jehovah's Witnesses who haunted our 'hood presumed we were black Baptists and left well alone.

'That's how you tell if someone grew up middle class,' I wandered, 'whether their father knew what to do with the Catherine Wheel. Of course, we never had any pins in the house. We just used to bin it.'

'Your grandmother . . .' Dr Death prompted, drawing daffodils in my margins.

'My . . .' Grandmother. My gran. I said it in my head, and even unspoken it had the effect of making my brain open up, like a flower filmed in fast motion. In a way it couldn't have yesterday, with my mother calmly designing her decline and fall, with me keeping my eye on the ball and chain my mother sought to string around her neck. My gran, my one and only.

'My grandmother, Liza Sharp, was the only grandparent I ever had. Ever knew, rather. She's my father's mother. Somehow, I know this sounds bad, it seemed so right that the others had died before I was born.'

'How –' These Asians, you see, they're careful with their lives. They don't feel immortal like white people do.

'Oh, drink, cancer, drink and cancer, the curse of the cursing classes. Anyway, Liza was the only one left. Get this: before she married her husband, Mr Sharp, she was Liza Blount. Isn't that a scream?'

'A veritable hoot.' My Alibhai's throwing a moody

now, because I've dragged her through a bush, or rather a shrub, backwards. But that's too bad.

'Anyway, she must have been born in like the nineteen-tens. In the Seventies, when I was a teenager, she must have been in her sixties. D'you remember the Seventies, doctor?'

She gave me a dry look, trying to imply she'd been locked in a lavatory for the entire decade by her fire-breathing father. But look at her, with her career and her hardy annuals! If she was a slave of Islam, I was a slave of Satan. I'd guessed a long time ago, pretty damn accurately as it turned out, that Mr Alibhai was one of those hip Hindus who believes that educating a daughter is both money in the bank and finger in the face to dumb ideas of What Asian Girls Do.

I remembered my school, a semi-tough comprehensive. I remembered the Asian girls who suddenly appeared, out of Africa, victims of a racism not white but black. I remembered Niagla (was that how she spelt it?) who we had taught to say 'Bugger off!' to teachers. Of course, because of her frightening flight from Uganda, she had not been punished. But after that, I remember Niagla and her little sisters being totally accepted even by the swaggering, swanking ringleaders of my set, and I remember them standing by on the sidelines, smiling politely, while these savage suedehead swans bullied ugly white girls so crassly that even I turned away.

'You came from Uganda?'

She frowned, like I'd said, 'You come from Catford?'

'My family. Go on.'

'Well, the Seventies: it wasn't just hotpants and Harold Melvin, you know –'

'Harold Wilson,' she said testily. I hate that. Someone thinking I'm that stupid, like I thought Harold Melvin was PM. And Dennis Law helped him soak the rich.

'Harold Melvin *and* his band the Bluenotes,' I pointed out. 'Well, it wasn't just that. It was that long, shimmering, sunlit bit of the century, after the Pill but before AIDS. It was a great time to be a kid, amongst other things. With all that to look forward to.'

'Smorgasbord, indeed.' People really don't have any idea, do they, how unattractive sulking looks from the outside?

'So I was like, a kid then. I was an only child, but I had a lot of cousins. And we all adored Gran. Worshipped her. She was the parents we wanted. The parents we dreamt of. You know like most kids go through a period of hating their parents and fantasising that they're adopted? Well, we never needed that. We had Liza.'

Dr Alibhai struck out for the shore, speaking decisively. 'She gave you the love your parents withheld. She was warm, and nurturing.'

'Oh, NO!' I turned my face to her, and I could feel my own glow. I could taste salt, for the first time in a low-sodium decade, and I knew the tears were not for Liza, who was alive, but for Nicola, who was dead – Undead? You tell me. But not for long. 'Oh, NO. She was *bad*.'

Liza's house was in Victory Street, which was in an extremely 'rough' bit of Bristol. Note quotation marks, reader! This is because it was precisely the 'rough' parts of Sixties cities whose citizens felt quite normal about leaving their doors unlocked. I'm not doing a good-old-days-thing here; I'm stating a fact. In Victory Street, if you locked your front door they thought you were a total slag with something to hide. For some reason they pulled these houses down in the Seventies and stuck the citizens in tower blocks. I think this is what's known as black humour.

Cleanliness was next to godliness in these houses – but so long as you showed a squeaky-clean doorstep you could get away with a multitude of sins behind closed doors. So far as I could make out, the working class of my grandmother's generation had what I can only call a music-hall morality. 'There's no harm in it!' 'A little of what you fancy does you good!' If a crime didn't have a victim, then it wasn't really a crime. This is pretty damn cool, especially when practised by people with no teeth.

And this is why there were six school-age Sharps in my grandmother's parlour at two p.m. on a Monday. We sat scattered around the floor, watched over by the dainty ornaments and seaside souvenirs who strained for a view over the cold shoulders of emptied beer bottles and cider flagons, waiting to be taken from whence they came. A blue budgerigar flew around the room displaying a sense of urgency and purpose that could only be phoney. The windows were open – but no one ever wanted to leave Liza's. He came to rest on her shoulder, on her shawl, where she sat in the room's only armchair.

Liza had the regulation white hair and pink cheeks that put a girl out of the sexual bring-and-buy, but her blue eyes were unusually shrewd and her hands had a life of their own. They moved around her lap like ferrets. She was drinking rum and blackcurrant from a pint glass with a Guinness chaser, and scoffing from a huge twist of humbugs while she watched the wrestling on TV. My cousins and I sat serenely pulling strings through brown paper bags. This was Liza's work, and if I told you how much it paid per hour you wouldn't believe me.

She leans forward in her chair, all spite and saliva. 'Pull 'is 'ead off, Mangler. Crush 'is wotsits.' Made reckless by malice, she leans too far forward and falls on her face to the carpet. With speed and syncopation but with no alarm, the six of us move in and winch her back on to her throne. We've borne witness to this scene many times before.

'Mind yourself, Gran!' says little Nicola, bless her Popsox.

'Where's the ref? Swindle . . .' moans Liza. She swigs from her glass and tries to replenish it, but the half-bottle of Morgan's is empty. 'Kim, my lover, Gran's med'cine's gone. Nip down the bottle and jug and get I some more. On the slate. Bless thee.'

Kim, who's thirteen if she's a day, skips to it. Liza looks around with some satisfaction, inspecting her troops. 'Right – that's Kim, Kevin, Darren, Warren, Steph and Nicky. My little Nicky.' Her claw moves through my silky hair, causing me much pain and pride. Well, *obviously* I'm her favourite. ''Ang on. Where's our Christine?'

'She's at school, Gran,' says Steph self-righteously.

'School!' Liza snorts. 'That's how it starts!'

'How what starts, Gran?' asks Kevin, no loss to the Brains Trust.

'Never you mind.' Liza's eyes light on two strapping lads of fourteen. 'Darren, Warren. When you up in front of the beak?'

'Tuesday next, Gran.' Darren's the mover and shaker here, note.

'I'll be there, then.' Liza makes a *moue*, though she couldn't spell it. 'Put you in care, would they? Wire waistcoat school, we used to call it. As if you b'ain't in your old gran's care already.' She turns her humbug bag upside-down. 'One out, all out. Warren, go down Giles's and get me a quarter of 'am off the bone. Darren, borrow us some 'umbugs when 'is back's turned. And don't get caught or –' Liza takes a huge old-fashioned poker from the fireplace and puts it into the fire. It comes out glowing red like a moral absolute – 'thee'll feel this.'

We stare at it, terrified to the point of titillation. She's done this a hundred times, and it always feels real.

'Right, Gran.' Warren can't take his eyes from the poker as he and Darren exit walking backwards, stumbling over their feet and each other. They're the toughest boys in the big playground, but with Gran they're blushing jelly.

Dr Alibhai's hiding it well, but I can tell she's pretty thrown by this little bit of living history. 'But she never actually assaulted Warren and Darren with the poker, did she?' Then she remembers who's paying for her shrubfest. 'Or *you*?'

I'm lying on my back on her couch, but I feel as

though I'm lying on a beach in the sun. My hands are linked behind my head and my legs are crossed in a profoundly Vargas way. My hair's come loose and I'm (for once) so relaxed that I *know* I'm relaxed. I speak like I'm hypnotised, or in love.

'You know, doctor . . . it's weird. I was talking to my cousin Steph about this years ago, and we worked out that while we all – the cousins – seem to have a *memory* of being – well, *branded*, if that's your take on it, none of us have a mark. And none of us remember seeing it happen to anyone else. Do you know what?'

'What?' Dr Alibhai says it like she really doesn't want to know.

'I think we just *wanted* it to happen.'

She's shaken, so much so that she drops her shrubs. 'Surely not!'

'Oh, not in any sort of kinky, masochistic way,' I say airily. And believe me, I know about these things. I've spent a not inconsiderable amount of my one and only life chained to the Baby Belling or the microwave. ('It's great how long you and Matt have been together,' people are always saying. You try leaving someone when you're handcuffed to the rotisserie.) 'Just to belong to her – because we loved her so much. We would have done anything for her. And she would have done anything for us.'

Pick a day, any day so long as it was a schoolday, and you'd find the young Sharps sprawling on the floor at Liza's faintly fetid feet, swigging Tizer and scoffing Smith's crisps. I, golden-haired little Nicky, was usually to be found lying on my stomach in the pride of place, drawing, my nose only inches from those hideous feet, whose corns were so extraordinarily well developed that her shoes had to be mutilated copiously in order to accommodate them. You've heard of peep-toe shoes? My gran wore peep-corn jobs.

I hold up my drawing. 'Do you like it, Gran?'

Liza peers at it suspiciously. 'What is it? S'all squiggle!'

'It's not a thing. It's a mood.' Get me, wasn't I the cutest? 'I call it "Ambience".'

Liza shakes her head decisively. 'What's that when it's at 'ome? They didn't 'ave it when I was a wench, thass for sure.'

Steph shouts suddenly from her lookout perch. 'Gangway! Auntie Teresa at twelve o'clock! Coming this way!'

'But it's *two* o'clock,' protests Cousin Kevin, bless him. He's not trying to be funny, either.

Kim shoves him, jumping up. 'Get on your feet, you moron!'

We move fast, having evacuated the parlour many times before, and always successfully. Drinks, sweets, Smith's crisps, school satchels and Sharp kids pile out of the room and up the stairs into Liza's bedroom.

Knock knock, who's there? It's Teresa, my mother, none other. She's a tall dark handsome number, slightly tired and anxious-looking but, hey, she's a mother, she likes it that way! She looks a little out of place in Victory Street, where the women consider curlers to be headgear suitable for all occasions, like hats and scarves elsewhere, and she walks a little too quickly for comfort.

Teresa peers in at the window, a low habit but one she can't quite break herself of. Liza sits serenely watching television. Teresa raps on the window and Liza smiles, going to open the door.

''Lo, my love.' She shuffles back to her parlour and Teresa follows her. She always looks somewhat suspicious around Liza, the cow. Well, of course, as it turned out, she had good reason to. But that's not the point! 'Why dissn't thee tell me thee was coming?'

'Why, Liza, would you have baked a cake?'

'Got a nice jam roll from Giles. Don't like 'omemade cakes. Don't taste real, some'ow.'

'I just felt like surprising you, Liza.' Teresa perches on the arm of something – she's big on perching. 'Why – expecting visitors?'

''Aven't seen a soul all day.' Liza stares at her beadily, almost inviting contradiction. 'Cuppa tea?'

'Thanks. My feet are killing me.' No, Mother! *No!* Your *shoes* are killing you! There is a slight, technical difference, I think you'll find!

Teresa clocks the room, looking for clues. 'Liza, you haven't seen anything of Nicola these past few weeks, have you?'

'Every weekend, my wench,' calls Liza from the kitchen. 'With you and Tom.'

'No – I meant during the week.'

Liza comes in carrying a tray bearing tea and Jammy Dodgers. I like to think that these are a visual pun, considering the conversation. Her manner is slightly amused. 'But Nic's still at school, b'ain't she? In the week? Only a titchy tart still.'

Teresa takes her tea testily. 'Liza, please don't use that word.'

'What word?'

'Tart.' Teresa drinks her tea and burns her tongue.

Liza smirks. 'Why not?'

'Because it doesn't mean what it used to mean when you were young. It means –'

'What?'

'You know.'

'No.'

'Well – prostitute.'

'What's wrong with being a prostitute?' Liza demands indignantly. 'I've been one all my life – and my mother too, and her mother before her! I had that padre from St Patrick's over trying to get me to go to 'is Black Mass – and I told 'im, I did, we've always been prostitutes in my family. You should 'ave seen 'im run! 'Eld up his skirts and legged it!' She laughs like a drain (she smells a bit like one too, but what the hell, I love the bitch).

My mother puts down her cup and stands up. 'You do it on purpose, don't you, Liza?'

'Do what, my wench?'

'Never mind.' She picks up her handbag. 'Nicola's been missing school. Steph too, and Kim and the boys.'

'Little 'orrors!' Liza's wrath is dreadful to behold. 'Give them this, I will!' She takes up her poker and brandishes it with some relish. It knocks over a waste-paper basket, and a way lot of empty Tizer cans roll out.

Teresa looks at them, then at my gran. 'Been on the Tizer, Liza?'

But Liza is looking past Teresa to a chair, which proudly displays my ambitious crayonned abstract. Teresa follows her gaze, goes to it and picks it up.

'What's this?'

Liza looks her in the eye, so cool. 'I call it "Ambulance".'

Teresa sighs and puts the drawing down gently. 'I'd better go.' Liza follows her into the hall. 'And if you do see Nicola, or any of them . . .'

Liza brandishes the poker once more. 'I'll make 'em bump back! Their nasty little feet won't touch the ground!'

But something smart in Teresa knows that Liza is brandishing the poker at her; knows that Liza is saying, in her very sophisticated and covert code, 'Get out, you boring bitch, with your bourgeois aspirations, before I knock your block off! Those kids are mine, blood of my blood, working-class blood royal, and they're living the way my people have always lived! It's you, you, that's out of step! So back off!'

Teresa turns her back and walks to the door.

There is a loud burp, Technicolor in its vulgarity, from upstairs.

Teresa turns back and looks at Liza.

Liza has her hand to her mouth, and she says demurely, 'Beg pardon. Bleedin' Tizer.'

Teresa closes the door behind her.

Liza smiles with saturnine satisfaction. Then she walks to the foot of the stairs, puts two arthritic fingers in her mouth, and whistles up her troops.

Chapter **Three**

I'm back with my very good friend the head-shrink, and she's looking at me like she's about to offer me a refund. Is it really so shocking, my story? Worse than being chucked out of Uganda and being accused of eating cat food? People don't *hear* about the working class, you see – it's that 'We are the people of England, who haven't spoken yet.' Come on – it's a bit of truancy and a putative branding. It's not so much.

'My dad was one of five brothers – dig it, that was a small family then! And another three died at birth, the usual thing. Liza's husband, Daniel, was a tyrant, apparently. Not that I'm judging the guy: it was their culture, wasn't it? When he got home from work, after stopping off at the local hostelry no doubt, for like three hours, he wouldn't go straight into the house; he'd stand on the doorstep and whistle. That meant Liza had to get his grub on the table and the kids into bed! Amazing, isn't it – like Thingy von Trapp in *The Sound of Music*.'

'Most amazing.' She's still screwing her shrubs. I'm using 'screwing' in the Cockney sense, 'to look hard at', here. In case you wondered.

'Christos, that was *my* family!' I sit up straight, shocked. 'That could have been *me*, being whistled at! Like some *dog* or something!'

'Nicola, the only man who would dare whistle at you would be at least fifty feet up a scaffolding.'

'Yeah, but just think!' I'm really having breakthrough thoughts here. 'I'll tell you what: when I think about my family – my history, if you like – I feel as though I'm standing on top of this very tall building, looking down. I get this sort of . . . vertigo. Vertigo, that's it. The past makes you dizzy, doesn't it? It's like a fairground ride that never ends. Just gets faster and further away.'

'You certainly are on form today, Nicola. Things better with Matt?'

'He's in Mauritius. On a shoot. But it makes you think, doesn't it? I mean, we go on about Islam and everything, but it was all happening here about fifty years ago! Which admittedly is an incredibly long time, but –'

'I doubt that the shariah laws ever made it as far west as Somerset, Nicola,' she says, dead snooty.

'It's Avon County now,' I sidestep smartly. 'But you know what I mean. Anyway – it was a relief to everyone when the old guy bought the building.'

'The house in Victory Street, you mean?'

I laugh. 'No! Like, kicked it. Swinging with the majority. Dead, if you want to be a downer about it. Where was I? Well, Gran had to leave school when she was twelve to go and work in this cotton factory. It wasn't no art school, put it that way. Married at eighteen. All those kids, all those kids dying. No money, natch – used to take her wedding ring to the pawnbroker's every Monday and get it back every Friday, payday. But when the old guy died, she became the head of the family, and it was like all of us knew that was the way it was always meant to be. And suddenly it was the Sixties, and everything was sunny, and there was suddenly all this money about. Every weekend, my dad and all his brothers took their families to Liza's, and every single day one of the brothers or their wives called in on her – and of course, we kids were always there. She was waited on hand and foot. She lived like a queen. She had a budgerigar called Lux –'

'Was he white?' Dr Alibhai asks, with what seems to be a genuine and rather oddball interest.

'No, blue. But, like I say, things just seemed really good at this time. For kids, thinking about the big sky-blue future; for teenagers, shagging away like it was going out of fashion. (Which it was about to, only they didn't know that.) And for old people like my gran, for whom against all odds and experience life suddenly began to get better. Just think of it! She had all the reassurance of her stuff from the old world – her house, her street, her family – with all the comforts of the new: television, wrestling, the welfare state. She was in her element, at last. She was the one person I think I've ever known who was completely at home in the time and the place she found herself in. That's why she was so great to be with.'

'I see.' Lying sow. She shuffles her papers, trying to shake off her shrubomania. 'And how does your grandmother feel about her environment now?'

That's it. My bubble is burst, my pout is pursed. The dream is over and I sit up, shamed. 'I don't know,' I admit. 'I left Bristol in the Seventies; by then the house in Victory Street had been pulled down and she was living in a flat. She still left her front door open, apparently, like she had in the old neighbourhood. Everyone tried to make her lock it. But she never would. And nothing bad ever happened to her. Because her karma was so great . . .'

'Her karma.' The doctor is drier than Iran. 'I see.'

I get stroppy. 'In fact, the only bad stuff she suffered didn't come from strangers but from her own sons. A bunch of Judas goats if ever there was one. They got into their own lives more, foreign holidays and dinner-dances and what have you, and Liza became less and less the centre of things. Because the flat was so small . . . that's the excuse they used, anyway. Self-absorbed bastards.'

'When was the last time you actually saw your grandmother, Nicola?'

I thought about it, and then I didn't want to think about it, and then I said it. 'Seven years ago.' My God, even she looked shocked. 'But I was her *favourite*. And there's always been that *bond* between us that just doesn't *need* anything as artificial as physical proximity to keep it together. Do you understand what I'm trying to say, doctor?'

Then she smiled at me with real, gratis warmth, and she said, 'Why don't you call me Usha?'

I sat on the train in a first-class carriage, utterly vacant, staring out the window as Berkshire became Wiltshire and Wiltshire became Avon. Avon! Where did they get that from, when it's at home? It's a bloody cosmetics company! Ding-dong – Avon calling! The *cheek*!

When we're the absolute *heart*, no, *source* of England! King Arthur, and Cary Grant, and all that jazz! It's the Tall Poppy Syndrome, isn't it? Take Camelot and turn it into Camay. You can't argue with people like that.

The paper I was pretending to read employed Zoë Heller, and turning to her column I remembered *my* Zoë, and what she'd said to me when she found out my plan.

'Nicole, you are insane. I mean that: you are literally, luridly, a lunatic. You are off your head. Out of your tree. Round the bend. Either that, or you cannot have thought logically about what you are saying. I'm sorry to bring this up, and I swore I never would, but do you remember the last time you tried to look after something? My lovebirds, when I was in Lithuania? They fucking *killed* each other!'

'It was a fucking lovers' quarrel!' I yelled at her. I'm pretty fragile these days. 'Seventy per cent of all murders are committed by cohabitees or former cohabitees! Those so-called lovebirds had it coming! It was nothing to *do* with me!'

'Nicole! Look at yourself, girl! Don't even bother to look in the mirror – just look at me! We are just not up to nurturing! We don't consume enough calories!'

'I am SICK of looking in the mirror!' I shouted. 'And I'm sick of looking into the mirrors around me, that are meant to be my friends! It's *boring* don't you understand? I'm fed up with living in a fucking buffet, just picking at stuff! I want something *real*!'

I thought I knew Zoë, but obviously I didn't. Obviously. Because she thought for a while and then she said – and this is just so nasty, and so untrue: 'Nicole. *Your* idea of *real* is Classic Coke.'

But here I am on the train, and that's pretty damn real. The coffee's crap, for instance. And believe me, the prospect of a blind date with my long-lost grandmother is not exactly a wanton wet dream.

My God, I've got to take her home with me!

And she'll still be there the morning after!

And the morning after that!

It strikes me suddenly that I truly may be a lunatic. But the terrible thing is that *it doesn't matter*. It's too late now.

All around me men get to grips with laptop computers and mobile phones. I stare at them hungrily. It's not them I desire, though; it's the luxury of their complete alienation. Often, especially when we're very young, we think we want to fuck men when what we really want is to *be* them. But we don't have penis envy, it's not some sexy dyke action number; we have Access envy, automata envy, AA envy. We want to be that dumb and disengaged. It is a rare woman who lives an unexamined life, despite the apparent bovinity of the breeding process; but even the most intellectual of men can easily lead lives free of moral anguish or doubt.

'Well, it's Sylvia Plath and Ted Hughes, isn't it?' Lucy said when I mentioned this.

'Bloody right!' I said. Memo: must learn a Sylvia Plath poem by heart. As for Ted Hughes, we did him at school. It's pretty depressing stuff; no wonder she did herself in.

I heard the voice of the woman I loved long before I saw her, and what a voice it was, too. Like a parrot, West Country born and bred (which means drunk), to which some human wretch with extremely cold hands was trying to do something unspeakable, probably sexual. I located the tableau from which the racket emanated – Teresa and Tom, my alleged parents, standing either side of her, stooping, talking in soft, insincere voices; she, Liza, sitting on a large lump of very cheap luggage, her dirty great handbag on her lap like it was growing there. Excuse me, but what exactly *is* a lap, when it's at home? And did more people have them in the past than have them now? Is a lap something you have or don't have according to your moral character and marital track record, or is it just a thigh thing? I mean, for example, could a multiple divorcee with a fairish coke habit really be said to have 'a lap'? As opposed to a laptop?

Anyway, whatever it is, Liza's got one. And I used to sit on it as if my life depended on it. And it does. More now than ever. I walked up to them. But they were so into their own little psychodrama that they didn't even see me.

'Just for a bit, Mum,' my father was saying, 'a little change'll do you good.'

'No, I tell thee!' My sweet silver-haired old granny. The human being I was just about to sacrifice a good chunk of my one and only life for. 'Leave me be! I b'ain't going off into the wide blue yonder with a tart I don't know from Adam! Anything might 'appen!'

I know it's really sad and girly, but I felt that horrible pain like someone's pulling a choke-chain of chitlin really tight round your throat. I blubbered up to her and indulged in a little light non-specific pleading.

'Gran!' I squatted down in front of her and clutched at her hands where they were clamped down on her handbag. She lifted the handbag and hit me round the head with it. I fell over backwards, seeing stars and remembering that she always carried a can of Guinness in case of emergency (i.e. not being within heaving distance of a Guinness outlet). I struggled to my feet but kept my distance this time, dancing around just out of her reach like a really bad boxer. 'Gran, it's me, Nicola. Nic. Nic-Nic. I was your favourite grandchild! Remember?'

'Remember what?' She swiped out at me with her handbag again. I pranced backwards and right on to the feet of a black guard, who swore at me. I saw my parents sniggering, racist scum. I pranced back up to Gran.

'The house in Victory Street? The poker! Lux the budgerigar? Shoplifting from Giles . . .'

'Oi! *Police!*' Liza yelled at the top of her rancid old lungs. 'There's a thief over 'ere! Self-confessed!'

'But I did it all for *you*, Gran!' I pleaded, near tears. 'You used to *send* me shoplifting . . .'

I had the brief and shallow but undeniably sweet sensation of seeing my mother wince at the revelation of her only daughter as a child criminal.

'I never did!' lied Liza loudly. 'Ooo! No wonder your nose is so big, my lady!'

Teresa recovered her composure and smiled smugly. 'Yes, well, that's all water under the bridge now.'

My dad chuckled. 'Or rum in your case, Ma!'

'The thing *is*, Nicola,' smirked Teresa, 'that your grandmother would obviously prefer to stay here. Where she *knows* people.'

'Excuse me, Mother.' I drew myself up to my full height and bridled extensively. 'But exactly who does my grandmother know at the Frau Crippen Home for the Elderly, Infirm and Vulnerable?'

There are no flies on Liza, and she's on this like a duck on doughboys. ''Ome? What 'Ome?'

Teresa looks daggers at me, then feathers at Liza. 'Now, Mum, we've *talked* about this. It's not what you –'

But Liza is on her feet and feeling no pain by now. No, I'm feeling it instead as she gives her suitcase one final hoist and slams it on to me. I'm still staggering under its weight even as Liza hightails it towards the waiting train.

'Come on!' she calls back urgently over her shoulder, what there is left of it. 'Look sharp!' I linger for one last moment over the slack, moronic jaws of my parents as they witness my last-minute triumph. 'They'll 'ave two gunny sacks over our 'eads and us both shipped off to the funny farm over Barrow Gurney if we 'ang about!' She scuttles up the steps and on to the train. All mine. I turn to bid a magnanimous farewell to the people who raised me.

I can't help smirking. A rich, urbane, see-you-around smirk. 'So it looks like it's *ciao* – Ma, Pa. I'll give you a bell when she's settled in. Nothing to worry about now, though. Everything under control.' My smirk threatens to eat my face and make a start on my neck for afters. 'Everything shipshape and Bristol fa –'

Teresa completely loses it now and steps forward with what can only be called a snarl. My father restrains her. 'Nicola,' she spits, 'everything *was* under control until you stuck your oar in.'

'Now, Treez . . .' my dad mollifies.

Teresa shakes him off, but buys it. 'You're right,

Tom. Nicola knows best, after all. She always has done, ever since she learnt to speak. Her first word was "no". Nothing's changed.' She sticks out her hand. 'Good luck.' There's a pause. 'You're going to need it.'

'Cheers,' I say airily. 'But I strongly doubt that. When you possess both compassion and efficiency, luck is rather immaterial.'

'Oi!' Liza yells through the train window. 'You! Where's me stuff? There ain't a pot to piss in on this charabanc!'

'Coming, Gran!' I call, struggling off with her suitcase. Behind my back I feel my parents exchanging Looks, which are apparently what you start exchanging instead of bodily fluids after you've been married for that long.

As the Paddington train pulled into Bath Spa, I staggered back to our seats laden down with 'refreshments' – though you really don't feel refreshed after stuffing yourself stupid with Cheddar Ploughman's sarnies and double G&Ts, do you? You just feel more knackered. Why is this? – to find Liza sticking her tongue out at a little boy on the platform with his leg in plaster. He hobbled away, backwards, still looking at her, amazed. Then he walked into a trolley, keeled over and began to cry. His mother ran up to him, hauled him to his feet and slapped him.

Liza sniggered.

I started to say something, then remembered that she'd grown up in a different culture to me. Casual racism, wrestling to the death and branding blood relations with red-hot pokers was all in a day's work when she was a girl. So I didn't say anything. Instead I sat opposite her and smiled as I handed her her tea.

'Here you go, Gran – three sugars! Live dangerously, eh?'

She scowled at me. 'What biss thee talking about, wench?' Then she scowled at the tea.

'Whass *this*?'

'It's tea, Gran.'

'Where's me saucer?'

'There isn't one.'

'But I always drinks me tea out of me saucer!' She looked at my paper plate, which bore the Sandwich of the Week, and in an instant, like a conjuror's, her claw-like hand had whisked the plate out from under. My Sandwich of the Week hit the ground and was a memory. 'Giss! Ta very much.'

'Gran!' I wailed like a child.

She poured a little tea on to the plate and attempted to trickle it from the plate into her mouth. The plate buckled, spraying tea over Liza, the table and me.

'Ow, I'm ruined!' This was a blatant falsehood, protected as she was by layers of man-made clothing. 'Get some bicarb, quick!'

'Gran! Look at you!' I jumped up, grabbed at the pathetic couple of paper napkins Great Western Railway do you the honour of exchanging with you for the arm (one) and the leg (one) you pay for your first-class ticket, and attempted to mop her lap (remember that?) off. Quick as a flash, she reaches over me, grabs my sandwich memory from the floor of the train, dunks it into her tea and takes a bite. It's Wild Salmon With a Mild Curry Mayonnaise, for the love of Mike! 'Waste not, want not!'

'Gran!' I wail again, and up walks the ticket collector.

'Tickets please, ladies.'

'Oh, yes! Yes, of course!' I began to root in my bag in that guilty way you do.

The collector is eyeballing Liza's lap, which is wet, and her front, which is covered in liquidised Sandwich of the Week. 'Are you in trouble, madam?'

Liza glares at him. 'Don't thee be disgusting – my 'usband's been dead these thirty years. And don't call me "madam". The nerve.' She picks a bit of salmon from the front of her coat and pops it into what she thinks is her mouth. But it's her right nostril.

'Here you are, um . . . officer,' I gush, thrusting two tickets at him. I'll tell you one thing about the combination of being of working-class origin, of 'respectable' status and taking a wagonload of Class A drugs: it makes you respectful as all get out towards anyone wearing a uniform. I've been known to practically genuflect towards park keepers, which really makes my snooty gal pals like Lucy and Emma laugh like drains.

'I'm sorry, madam,' he says, examining them, 'but these are second-class tickets. And you're occupying a first-class compartment. Would you like to move, or pay the difference?'

'Pay the difference,' I said hurriedly. I can think of a few things more gut-churningly embarrassing than having to relocate to a second-class compartment and settle in amongst the natives when I've spent the previous half-hour sashaying back and forth to the buffet, toilet and for all I know the guard's van for a quick snog with the almost audible aura of the first-class passenger – but being stripped naked and dragged through the Groucho Club wearing nothing but a double-headed dildo and a large scarlet letter A isn't one of them. But hey, I'm funny that way.

But Liza puts her hand – her *claw* – over my hand. ''Ang on. What biss thee doing?'

'I'm paying the difference, Gran,' I hiss.

'Paying the piper, more like!' she snorts. 'And it'll go straight into 'is pocket, if I'm not mistaken! Look at 'is eyebrows! "Beware of 'e 'ose eyebrows meet – for in 'is 'eart there lurks deceit!" Bible,' she adds devoutly, before revving up again. 'Oy, 'Itler! Why d'you think we fought the war?'

'Well, it certainly wasn't so malicious old biddies like you could exploit fare-paying passengers, madam,' comes back the collector, quite cleverly I think. 'My father fought with the International Brigade – *and* he lost a leg in Italy.'

'Thass funny, innit?' says Liza sociably, her righteous rage forgotten. 'Cos Italy's shaped like a leg. "Long-legged Italy kicked poor Sicily" – 'Ere, maybe that was the one 'e lost!' She cracks up at her own wartime wit and wisdom, and I consider fleeing through the compartment, wrenching open a door and flinging myself from the speeding train.

Instead, I start apologising. Natch. I could apologise for western Europe. 'Oh, officer, I'm so sorry. She's eighty-five, you know . . .'

'Really? She doesn't seem a day over eight.' He fixes me with a beady glare. 'And don't call me "officer".' He walks off.

I look at Liza. Bits of salmon are falling from her nostrils on to the table and she's looking at them with interest, like they're manna from heaven, before attempting once more to stow them in the right part of her face. 'Oh, Gran.' I can't help saying it. 'What's happened to you?'

'Nothing's 'appened to me.' She stares out of the window, her lip stuck out, only it's not a pout – when does pouting become a physical impossibility for women, like an erection for men? She looks as rebellious as hell, as me, as any teenager wishing fields of fire on the dumb green thing that's holding them back. 'It wouldn't dare.'

Chapter **Four**

We're in the taxi going to my place, so of course this gives Liza a whole new landscape to pick holes in. Not that somebody hasn't started the job for her already, I'll grant you. The way the taxi jolts going over the potholes, it's somewhat amazing that there's been one live birth that wasn't a home confinement to any woman living in the capital city over the last quarter-century. Personally I fail to see how the abortionist continues to do such a thriving trade while our roads are such one-way freeways to miscarriage.

I try to see London through Liza's eyes, and I start wishing I had her cataracts – the noise, the overpopulation, the sheer *aggression* of the place. No kidding, London makes New York look like Old York these days.

Liza stares at the strangely arrayed people with the eyes of a child; and by the way, that's not 'child' as in Mabel Lucie Attwell, that's 'child' as in *Lord of the Flies*. She nudges me as a bronzed boy on a bike, wearing one of those wussy masks over his mouth, comes level with us. He looks like the boy bride of some Muslim homo.

'Look! You've 'eard of the Flying Doctor – it's the Biking Doctor!' She leans forward and snaps back the partition, yelling so loud the driver really does jump. 'Oi! Knock 'im off 'is bike!'

I shrug apologetically at the young man, a sort of isn't-she-wonderful-for-eighty-five shrug. But he isn't having none, and when he stares back at me his eyes above the mask are literally crossed with fear. He *is* a wuss. Gran can smell the fear on people, see.

She sees Arabian babes in long black chadors. (I'm not being nasty, but is it any coincidence that it's the world's most unattractive female race who have been told by their male rulers that they have to cover up every inch of their face and body? I mean, you can't imagine the head of China saying: 'Oi! All you ugly Chinese bints with your soft beige skin and hairless bodies and lovely black bobbed does! Cover it up, will you? What d'you think the rest of the world's gonna think of us?' Or some West African chieftain: 'Hey, girls! With the big pouty lips and the long legs and those necks like a swan who's into stretch classes? Put it away, for the love of Mike! How d'you expect us to look the white man in the eye?' No – it's your Arab babe, with her handsome moustache and cowboy legs, who's been told to cover up.

I'd like to point out, by the way, that this is in no way racist. It's an *aesthetic* thing. I mean, *come on*, I'm an *artist*. I can't help noticing stuff like who's wearing what on her upper lip this season. I actually did once say to Zoë, offhand, that I thought chadors had a kind of minimalist elegance. You'll never guess what. She slapped me!

'Nicole, that's women's *lives* you're talking about!

Clothes aren't just clothes, you know!' I'll tell her that next time I call for her to go clubbing, and she's wearing a cut-off skin-tight T-shirt with JUNKIE WHORE SEX TARGET written on it.)

'Loada nuns round 'ere, in't there?' Gran is babbling as she clocks the flock of fatwah followers. 'Nun today – and nun tomorrow!' She guffaws. I *think* that's what it's called.

I smile weakly, then feel ashamed of myself for being so bloody patronising. I start prattling on about my flat to put her off the scent. Not that she could ever smell anything above the reek of Algapan and Deep Heat which emanates from her hot and wizened little body, bless her. 'I really hope you'll like my place, Gran. It's in Docklands –'

'Iss on the docks?'

'Yes . . . you see, Docklands is one of the most fa –'

'Full of prozzies, is it?' She doesn't seem at all horrified at the prospect, the old rogue, just interested. I'm the one who's horrified, at this gross insult to the value of my desirable property.

'Certainly not!' Amazingly, I sound like my mother. 'It's a most, uh . . . respectable . . . uh, riverside . . . residence. Yes.' I'm really glad Zoë can't hear me now. 'Anyway, I took three days off work – though I do work from home, as you probably know, so I'll always be, like, there for you – to make it extra cosy. There's a beautiful view of the river – one wall is made entirely of glass – and a garden square where –'

'Got a telly, 'ave you?'

I stopped, mid-burble. 'Ye-es.'

''Ow big?'

Damn big. 'Big enough.'

'That's me sorted, then.' She settled back with a satisfied smirk. 'Got cable? WWF?'

'I haven't heard of that channel, but yes we do have –'

'Iss not a channel, stupid!' She cackled. 'Iss wrestling! On the cable!'

'Well . . . good. Gran, I must tell you about the feeling of community in –'

But Liza's eyes have alighted on the THANK YOU FOR NOT SMOKING sign. She nudges me.

'Gis's a fag.'

'But Gran, you don't –' Why do I bother?

'Gis's a fag or I'll get out in the traffic and buy some.'

I put a cigarette in her mouth and light it. I only ever do this as a flirtatious gesture, with men when sober and girls when drunk. It feels weird to be doing it with an eighty-five-year-old. You wouldn't want to snog one, would you?

You've guessed it. The cab driver clocks us and pulls back his partition like greased lightning moonlighting as a mean-minded petty bureaucrat. 'Thank you for not smoking, madam,' he says briskly to Liza.

This was what she wanted! She leans forward and scowls through the beautiful smoke, scowling with glee. 'Bugger off and buy yer own!' She slams the partition, turns to me and smiles like a depraved baby. She is wonderful. My heart becomes a Slush Puppy.

'Oh, Gran . . .'

He was the first cabbie I've had who wouldn't take a tip. 'I thank you, no,' he said, giving me the change I hadn't asked for. Liza's easily going to keep herself in Guinness at this rate.

In the cage lift going up, I feel nervous. Hamster stomach. Liza looks disapproving as I close the two metal doors.

'My sister Kate knew a woman once. In a contraption like this. Reached out through the metal and it took 'er 'and off.'

I don't know, what do you say to an urban myth? 'Myth off'? I try to be bright and sensible. 'But Gran, you wouldn't ever do anything so silly, would you?'

Liza makes a Gene Vincent face. 'Depends,' she says moodily. Depends on what, for the love of Mike?

The lift stops. 'Here we are,' I say cheerily. I take her suitcase and open the grilles. Liza follows me out and we walk towards my front door. I unlock it and stand back, ushering her in. 'Home sweet home.'

She's silent as I follow her in and close the door behind us. She looks around wonderingly for a full thirty seconds, then turns to me with a tiny smile. ''Ome sweet 'ome? If you'm a bleedin' crate of pilchards, per'aps!'

She takes off her hat – navy blue, soft, not chic – and walks around like an estate agent, only far more physically attractive. 'Is this what they call one of them squats, then? Cussn't thee afford a proper 'ouse on the money you'm making?'

I laugh merrily. Stupid old biddy. 'It's a *loft*, Gran.'

She scuttles over and picks up her suitcase. 'Is it? Well, where's the rest of the 'ouse? I'm not clearing out no loft for thee, I wants to put me feet up.'

I laugh a little less merrily. 'Not that sort of loft, Gran! It's a . . . conversion.'

Liza looks at the brace of brimming ashtrays offering up their bounty which frame my drawing board. 'Thass right? Not exactly an Immaculate Conversion, is it?' She indicates the board itself. 'Wass this when it's at 'ome?'

'That's my drawing board. Where I do my work.'

'Work!' She makes a nasty noise which begs a spitoon. Or a punch up the bracket. 'Scribbling, you mean.'

'Gran, if it pays the rent and it keeps you awake worrying at night, then it's work, believe me.'

She doesn't. She's on a roll. Liza looks at me, beautiful and triumphant. 'Twelve years old I was when I went to work in the cotton fact'ry. By the age of fourteen, my 'ands was like minced beef. Minced beef. Red raw.' She pauses, then smiles. ''Appy days . . .'

'Yes, well, Gran.' I'm brisker than I want to be. 'You're going to have to learn to live without the arcane pleasures of the daily acid dip now you'll be living here with me. You're going to have to learn how to pamper yourself, put your feet up a bit. Live a little.' I lead her towards the glass wall, towards the view. 'Now, here's the river –'

'A bit damp, innit?' She pulls away. 'Just looking at it brings back me old trouble.' She peers around. 'Where's me bed?'

I point at my bed. Matt's and mine. The marital bed. The sumptuous grave of all desire. 'There.'

'So where be yours?' she asks, really suspiciously. You'd think I was trying to have my way with her. Which I am, but *definitely* not sexually. Do me a favour. I may be a married woman, but I'm not *that* desperate.

I point to a door. 'In there.'

Liza goes to the door and opens it. Naturally, it's a cupboard which contains bedding materials. She turns to me and says incredulously, 'You'm going to sleep in a *cupboard*?'

'No!' I walk up behind her. 'On a futon. Look.' I point.

'Where's me privacy, then?' Liza looks around the loft, as if her privacy is an actual thing she can find.

I run, the creep, to the side of my big bed and roll out a quartet of long Japanese screens which surround it. 'Look at these, Gran! Aren't they beautiful? Japanese. *Very* reasonable. I found them in the Camden Passage –'

'I'll give you passage!' Liza scolds me insupportably. 'I can't do me bizness be'ind that! Iss paper! What if I put me foot through it?'

I've got to admit it; I'm exasperated. Quite frankly, if you ask me, it's a bloody wonder I'm not homicidal. 'Gran,' I plead, 'why are you being so difficult? *Why* are you attempting to play the part – and very badly too, if I may say so – of a silly old lady? I know you, don't forget. And I also know that the only time *you'd* ever put your foot through anything would be so you could kick the crap out of the poor bugger on the other side.'

Liza advances on me, instantly energised by the slightest sign of aggression, at least fifteen years falling from her like dead skin cells as she walks. 'Right. That's it, my lady. I've 'ad enough! You'm goin' to feel my –'

But I dance towards the door instead. *My* door. And I say: 'There isn't a poker – we've got underfloor heating. I'm going out to get us some dinner; I could pay you back for all this by tormenting your internal organs with Thai takeaway or chilli tacos, but I won't. I'll get you a nice Mild Cheddar sarni on white bread; it's going to be pretty hard to hunt down something so exotic, and damned expensive when I find it, but I have my spies and my savings.' I dodge through the door, then look back round it. I'm merciless. 'And, Gran, I strongly advise you to take this time to settle in. After all, you're going to be here quite some time. *Ciao*.'

She looks small and lonely as I close the door. But hey, I feel that way every day of my life. Now at last we've got something in common.

I am becoming a Monster.

Some people say Docklands is 'soulless'; excuse me, what does this mean? How on Earth can a place have 'soul'? How can you find 'soul' in bricks and mortar, buildings and streets? And, even more interestingly, what sort of soulless booby insists on his environment having 'soul'? It's *people* who are meant to have soul; if we're for some reason incapable of this, it's going it a bit to try and pass the burden on to our poor insentient neighbourhoods. It's like those people who insist on wearing slogans on their T-shirts, yet when you attempt to engage them in conversation they haven't got two thoughts to rub together. People *do*; things *are*. I may be more of a visual person than a verbal one, but even I've got that one worked out.

So Docklands is as good a place as any for me to live. It's got shops, and to me that makes it a neighbourhood, though unfortunately I've got neighbours too. But my life, like most people's I know, is the room where I work and taxis and the Wild West End. You'd be surprised how much of London, real, inner London itself, is actually a collection of dormitory towns. People live where they can afford to live, and play elsewhere; this is just as true of an alleged part of London like Stoke Newington as it is of an honest-to-God dorm like Ilford.

When I used to voice my dreams of coming to London as an innocent teen, my mother and father would mutter about the 'loneliness' and lack of 'community spirit' extant in our fair capital. Of course, the cretins couldn't see that this was red-rag-to-a-bull time to any solitary, embarrassed adolescent worth her salt. (What's that mean?) The sheer, molten, golden joy of not being known! Not being watched! Being born again just the way you wanted to be! The perfection of loneliness!

In fact, it didn't turn out that way. Before I took up with Matt the Knife and moved out to my riverside palazzo, I lived in a broom cupboard over a shop in Southampton Row. Now you look at Southampton Row; it's shops, isn't it? It's shops with traffic in the middle. It's central, it's commercial, it's solitaire heaven.

Wrong! Above those shops are hundreds of apartments, great and small. Now your neighbours are easy enough to keep at arm's length; you just stiff them. You don't need anything from them, do you? But the shopkeepers, that's different. You *do* need stuff from them, obviously. Obviously. I mean, I can live without the milk of human kindness any day, but I definitely need something to stick in my coffee when I awake. I was young and healthy, for goodness' sake; I needed cigarettes, vodka, Pot Noodles and all the other basic provisions. So I had to have some sort of relationship with the local shopkeepers.

When I say relationship, I meant like 'please' and 'thank you' and the occasional smile. Did I ever have the wrong number! I don't know if you've ever watched *Postman Pat*, this kids' puppet show, but it was very popular when I was at St Martin's and we'd smoked too much dope. Anyway, Postman Pat lives in this mythical English village called Greendale. There's about fifteen people in Greendale, so of course everyone's real tight with everyone else: Mrs Goggins, Alf Thompson, Miss Hubbard, Major Forbes, Mrs Pottage, the Reverend Timms.

Excuse me, did I say 'mythical'? Well, I was wrong! Because, within three weeks of moving into what I thought was my own little padded cell in the asphalt jungle, London West Central, in the roaring traffic's boom, I discovered that I had in fact moved to Greendale! Yes, Postman Pat himself was on a sabbatical, and the faces here were of varied hue, and not the queasy putty pink of the puppets. But hot damn if that community spirit, that *friendliness*, that (some would say) *pushiness* wasn't thicker on the ground than Hubba-Bubba.

Item: cute young guy at newsagent's next door asks me if I'm a model. Yes, I know! I couldn't believe it either. Goaded, I let slip I'm an art student. For some reason, this lights the touchpaper and from here on in the comic genius of David and his six co-workers knows no limits. Routinely, in front of up to twenty paying customers, I am asked if I've cut my ear off yet. I'm asked, with mandatory leer, if I 'do nudes', and if so where do I put my brushes? One of the brighter employees seems particularly interested in 'action painting', and repeatedly enquires, like twice a day, whether I am wont to strip off my clothing, cover myself in paint and roll about on a large sheet of paper. Just passing the shop, I am regaled with cries of 'Oi! Picasso!' I end up in the surreal position of walking through three streets to get a pint of early-morning milk rather than go next door and become part of the living, breathing London story.

You might say, 'Oh, they were just sexists! Harassing a single woman!' But they weren't. Three of the gang were women, and two of those were black. And besides, I saw this routine pulled with so many people, most of them men. Exhausted young doctors were mercilessly teased about cold stethoscopes and being struck off for sexual misconduct. Earnest young lawyers suffered through light-years of banter about 'briefs' and exactly what they wore under their gowns. I once saw a vicar vomit on the shop floor from sheer nerves after a sustained campaign of insinuation vis-à-vis the Virgin Birth. There was a shocked silence before they sent out for sawdust, and I realised that this apparent tormenting of certain customers was actually meant as a compliment. We were regulars, in a city of randomness, and this constant reference to the hilarity of our professions was a rather manic, but basically well-meaning, gesture of recognition. In a small community, such incessant harping on our individual identity wouldn't have been necessary; here, for some reason, it was.

David and his posse cooled it for a few days after the vicar incident, and I felt that it was actually safe to venture back into their shop. For a handful of mornings my life was much easier, without the dawn trek to Lord Rayleigh's farm. And then, somewhere around the fifth day of sobriety, I was queuing up to pay for my booty when I sensed something about to blow, and big, with this troupe of too-long-frustrated comedians. David and Claudine, his main feed, kept catching the other's eye, and then looking towards one of us punters with one united gaze. Then they'd snap out of it and glare crankily at each other, like illicit lovers blaming the other one for putting temptation in their way.

I really thought we were safe when a young nurse from the Middlesex who I knew by sight from seeing her in the shop came in. I don't know if you've seen people who've been up all night on drugs trying to go out and function the next day; well, it doesn't matter a bit whether they've brushed their teeth, combed their hair and shined their shoes – they're *different*. The texture of their skin is different, their eyes are different, their movements are different. They seem not like a person, but like an alien pod trying to pass as a person.

That's the way this young nurse, Gita, looked. But she hadn't been doing drugs. She'd been doing life and death, and it showed. I don't know if she'd been working on a birth, or an abortion, or a painful death. But her wild eyes, and the purply sheen on her brown skin, signalled one thing: that she'd been out there the night before to a place where most of us won't go until we're forced there. And even when we're there, giving birth or dying, we won't really know what's happening because people like Gita will be doing our dirty work for us, and we'll be flying high on morphine. Well, she'd been there stone-cold sober, looking at the whole horrifying thing for twelve hours non-stop, and you could tell that it had driven her a little mad. But mad in that utterly selfless way that only nurses can do; all she wanted was a cup of tea and she'd be ready to go all over again.

I watched Gita go to the big refrigerator and look at the milk. She studied it too intently, as people deprived of sleep do. She smiled as she selected a pint of semi-skimmed, and it wasn't a pretty sight even though she was a pretty girl. She was smiling to keep from screaming.

I turned away, a bit spooked, and looked towards the counter. That's when I saw David and Claudine. They were staring at each other in a gauzy, giddy kind of way, like the lovers' first meeting in *West Side Story* when all the room disappears, and then they turned to look at Gita. She had joined the queue, holding her milk too tightly to her chest, her knuckles so tense and livid they looked like some new sort of ethnic jewellery. There must have been fifteen other customers in the shop.

Don't do it, I begged David and Claudine silently, please don't do it. I know you mean well. I know this is a city sort of love, some primal reaching-out through the stark terror of the modern world to show us that we're not really alone. But please, just let this girl, this Gita, this half-mad saint, be alone for once as she purchases her pint of semi-skimmed milk.

But David and Claudine were no longer in control of their actions. They were going to bring Greendale to

London West Central if it killed them. Claudine whispered something in his ear, and his face became that famous comic mask, the one who goes around with the depressed-mask guy.

''Ey, Gita . . .'

The queue turned to confirm his target. Gita leant forward with a slight smile, and I saw that her extremely short nails had somehow, through sheer force, pushed through the strong waxed paper of the carton. Milk ran down her front. It was like some creepy visual gag about woman the sustainer and nurturer of mankind. Almost, if it hadn't been for the fact that her eyes were like Charles Manson's.

''Ey, Gita . . . any chance of a blanket bath?'

Fifteen customers, well dressed, white and logical, fell instinctively to the floor as the scream filled the shop. It wasn't like any scream I've heard; it wasn't a scream of terror, or alarm, or excitement, or frustration. That is, it wasn't a scream which just happened, on the spur of the moment. No, hearing this scream you got the feeling that it had been worked on over an extremely long period of time. That it had squatted inside Gita both sternly and sensuously since she was about twelve years old, and that it had been royally fed: on racism, on sexism, on poverty, on a lousy inner-city education, on parental oppression, and finally on the almost surreal exploitation of the nursing profession in this country. It was a triumphant scream, almost visible, and I was reminded of filmic representations of Aladdin's genie bursting from his lamp, or Jesse Owens leaping from his starting blocks. It was the nearest I've ever come to liking opera.

'What the fuck . . .' The pint of semi-skimmed hit

David full in the face, and he collapsed on to a quivering Claudine, which was the nearest they'd ever get to sex as it turned out.

Her scream streaming out behind her like scarlet ribbons, Gita ran through the shop, the big handsome shop with its scented candles and its teddy bears and its million things a newsagent never had until now. Like all those cute little office things: executive desk toys, and Victorian-lady biscuits, and huge mugs, big enough to hold at least two pints of tea, with whacky things written on them. Like the one which Gita finally selects to smash over David's head as his eyes plead mutely for mercy, staring up into her born-again, beatific, beautiful face: YOU DON'T HAVE TO BE MAD TO WORK HERE – BUT IT HELPS!

I scored the cheese sarni after a fashion, and I felt like a real hunter-gatherer. I dragged it home by its hair and I scampered into the loft with a glee that practically begged for its come-uppance. Which came right on time.

I saw her there in the chair (Shaker, Quaker, whatever, Matt bought it, Mr House Beautiful – shame he's never home, but still), watching TV. Although the fixtures and fittings and soft furnishings were so different, I couldn't help it. It reminded me of Victory Street, and the way things used to be.

In the way things used to be, I pranced across the floor to her waving my mighty trophy, i.e. a mouldy cheese sandwich. 'Gran! Look what I've got you!'

Not moved, not moving, not taking her eyes from the screen.

'Leave me 'lone.'

Chapter **Five**

There's lots of unpleasant ways to wake up. With a hangover. With an uncircumcised man shoving his dick down your throat, hoping you won't notice: 'God – how did *that* happen? Sorry, I was just looking for the toilet.' With herpes, on the morning of that dream date with Daniel Day-Lewis. But if we're talking major alienation league, I maintain that one of the least pleasant ways of waking up is to the sound of a slammed door.

There's something about a slamming door that hurts, even if you're glad to see the back of the slammer. I guess it takes you back to when you were a surly teen, and the slamming door was the full stop on the end of every vicious skirmish with your parents. Or maybe your parents used to row a lot when your mother was in her thirties, and felt a last flaming desire to Get More Out of Life while she still could. This often led to her going with a small group of friends to the Over Thirties night at the Top Rank Suite, which believe you me is a shameless, knee-between-the-thighs-while-smooching-to-'This-Guy's-in-Love-With-You' meat market that makes the average teenage thrash look like a Quaker meeting. One of the friends had two different-coloured eyes and could get her hair into a chignon, so she was obviously bad news. And sooner or later, your father was going to put his foot down. Which he did by slamming a heck of a lot of doors.

Even when it doesn't sound angry, a slamming door seems at least sardonic, a sarky comment on your pathetic state of unconsciousness. My first reaction when I'm rudely awoken by one is to sit bolt upright and say, 'Who, me?' in a woefully guilty voice. That's what I did, and then I saw that the screens were awry and Gran was AWOL.

I jumped up and rushed over to the big bed. Not a sausage, or in Gran's case a saveloy. Just her dentures, pink and obscene, in a glass by the bed; marinating in Perrier, which she'd obviously mistaken for Pepsodent. In a brandy balloon, too. The sudden contrast between my world – the expensive glassware and the designer water – and hers – basically, ill-fitting dentures – suddenly struck me as the loneliest thing in the world, and I sat down on the rumpled bed and burst into tears.

I was crying so hard I didn't hear the door open or the corny old feet plod across the loft until she was right in front of me: 'What biss thee creating about?'

'Gran!' I stood up and went to fling my arms around her. She scowled and shoved me. I went sprawling on the bed.

'Well?'

'I thought you'd gone,' I snivelled.

'Bin shopping.' She gestured at the carrier bags around her feet. 'Took some money out your purse.'

'What did you buy?'

'Proper cleaning stuff. This place is a tip.' She picked up the bags and shuffled towards the kitchen.

'But I've got a cleaner . . .'

'Too right you 'ave.' She was at the draining board, sorting through her toxic purchases. 'And 'er name's Liza Sharp.'

'But Gran, I brought you here so that *I* could look after *you* . . .'

'Thass very nice for *you*, my wench.' She took the top off her Toilet Duck (is that a perverse name for a product, or what?) and sniffed the poisonous purple liquid approvingly. 'But what am *I* supposed to do all day? Pick me nose?' She looked around resentfully. 'Not that there's much to do 'ere once I've got that layer of filth off, though. Where's that 'usband of yours?'

I shuddered to think. 'Oh – he's abroad, working. He's away a lot.'

'Is that so?' She leant over the sink, sniffing at the plughole. Sometimes it seems that we're just a few years away from the primal sludge, doesn't it? Or in the case of my gran's nose at the moment, a few inches. 'Why 'aven't you got any kiddies yet, then?'

I laughed bitterly. 'Because I'm waiting for my husband to grow up and leave home,' I muttered.

'Is 'ee younger than you, then? One of these boy-toys?'

'No, he's the same age as me.' I started lining up her legion of cleaning fluids in the cupboard under the sink. 'Chronologically. But it's a bit like dog years and human years, isn't it, with men and women . . .'

'What sort of dog? I could fancy a nice Alsatian.

Comp'ny. Where'd you keep it?' She looked brightly around the loft.

I ignored her. I was getting used to the idea that I'd be doing a lot of this, or go stark staring nuts in record time. 'And now he's in Mauritius . . . getting off with some dopey little slag who thinks Verdi's some sort of pasta . . .'

'Who is? The dog?'

'No, Gran,' I said gently. 'I don't have a dog. I meant Matthew. My husband.'

Liza waddled out into the loft proper and went to the glass wall. She stared down at the Thames. It might have been the Nile for all the familiarity it had to her. 'Where's Mauritius, then?'

I shrugged. 'Somewhere in the Indian Ocean.'

Liza looked at me disbelievingly, then snorted. 'Gallivanting! Fat lot of good that'll do him!' She peered at me, in a distinctly value-judgemental way. 'Or you.'

'It's his *work*,' I said wearily.

'Taking nudie pictures? Nice work if you can get it!' Then I'm *positive* I heard her say under her breath: 'And I bet he does, too!'

'What was that, Gran?'

'I said, "I bet he misses you."'

I smiled gamely. 'Yeees . . .'

'Cheer up, my wench. You know what they say: "Absinthe makes the tart grow blonder."'

We stared at each other for a second, both attempting to make sense of this surreal shaft of wisdom. Then we burst into laughter, and for the first time since I'd got her home I felt that everything would be all right.

*

We had a great evening: I nipped out to Oddbins and got her some Guinness, and I found some Everton mints in a local newsagent's, and there was wrestling on Sky. She sat in the Shaker chair, which I had to pad out with pillows to stop her moaning – this, as you can imagine, looked completely hideous, completely bastardising the chair's stark beauty, but never mind – and I sat at her feet and it was real heart-in-the-mouth stuff, like when you're young and you're out with this boy you really have a vooly for ('vooly', from the Italian *volore*, to really want and have unrequited desire for, a bit like me and the person I'm married to, sick joke. But true! It's not until you marry someone that they can *really* evade, avoid or otherwise elude you) and you're counting the seconds until he puts his hand on your knee and you give him a Chinese burn because you've been told that men like girls to be Hard to Get. I've never been able to do this, you see. This is my big romantic problem. When I think someone's wonderful, it's all Lombard Street to a china orange that I'm going to turn to them with lovelight shining in my eyes and say breathlessly: 'I think you're wonderful and I'd really like to sleep with you.' For some reason which I've never been able to get my head around, this is about as attractive to a man who's about to seduce you as saying: 'I've got syphilis, piles and dog breath, and I'm married to a pathologically jealous psychopath. Would you like to sleep with me?' Men don't want you to be straight with them. It's true. They want you to run and hide and tease and flirt and withhold. Do this and they'll adore you unto death. And people say that women are masochists!

Anyway, there I was waiting for Gran to be so swept

away in the sheer emotion of the magic moment as the Undertaker pulls the head off Papa Shango that she'd put her gnarled old hand on my hair – and sure enough, fifteen minutes into the fight she did. True, her wizened claw tightened painfully on my silky locks as the on-screen tension built and, yes, I did find a modest amount of said hair on the floor afterwards when she was in the bathroom. But I didn't care. If there was any chance of regaining what we'd had all those years ago, I was ready to take my punishment and invest in a whole wardrobe of wigs.

So we had a few beers and Gran scalped me and it was just some enchanted evening. I put her to bed and – yes! Punches air! – actually dared to kiss her on the cheek and tucked her in and settled down in my futon to sleep the sleep of the just, or at least the just-scalped. I wasn't aware of anything else until I woke up a few hours later, and there was someone in the loft who hadn't been there when I put out the lights.

I just lay there with my heart playing 'Let There Be Drums' by Sandy Nelson and my eyes sort of bouncing off the ceiling on stalks. Then I heard the bed creak. Whoever it was, or how many, or armed with whatever, they weren't going to lay a hand on my gran and live to tell the tale. I threw caution to the winds, pulled my T-shirt down over my thighs, who true to form had decided to have a lie-in and get up ten minutes after the rest of me, and I was just about to run across the room with a Gita-type out-psyching scream when I heard a familiar male voice say:

'How does eight inches of salami grab you, served hot, with relish?'

Liza's voice came back, calm and considering. 'I could murder some chitlin. Plaited.'

'Oh Christ!' Matthew's voice cried. 'What *is* this?'

I switched on the light. The room really did look like a stage, and the men and women in it truly players in some gerontophile farce from hell. I, the wronged wife, aghast in my IF IT FEELS GOOD, DO IT! T-shirt. Matthew, the errant husband, wearing a suntan from Mauritius, a jaw down to his nipples and a disillusioned dick shrivelling like a dildo with a slow puncture. And between us, the third corner of the eternal triangle, my gran, fun-loving Liza Sharp, winceyette nightie up to her chin and her teeth out, gurning guilelessly in the bright light.

Liza stuck out her hand. Amazingly, she seemed amused by the whole thing. ''Ow do. Liza Sharp. Our Nic's grandmother. Whass your name again?'

'Matthew,' he gaped, and pulled a pillow against his shame, which was by now actually a bit too small for Liza to see at all, with her cataracts. 'Matt.'

'Welcome, Matt.' Liza cackled. 'Geddit?'

'I only wish I didn't,' my husband said wearily. He looked at me, and as he looked I felt these lust waves which made the room sort of shimmer, like when it's very hot in the summer, in a park . . . Excuse me, what am I babbling about? That's the effect he always had on me. I found him boring, I found him irritating, I found him middle class to the point of hiring-a-hitman daydreams. But I still couldn't be around him for more than fifteen minutes without having to get out of my wet underwear and into a dry hump.

I could see he was thinking the same, because his brown eyes were being slowly eaten by their black pupils until they were just these oily slicks of lust. I turned away, and I felt some sort of moisture roll down my inner thigh. I'd like to think it was sweat, because I can't bear to think my body would be such a traitor to me as to make it anything else. Please, leave me with my pathetic illusions of autonomy, will you?

'So. Liza, much-worshipped grandmother of Nicole. How long may we expect to enjoy the pleasure of your company?' Matthew's voice was directed at Gran, but I could feel his eyes on me. I could feel his eyes pull up my T-shirt, push me against the wall, mashing my nose against the exposed brick (I'd look a wreck tomorrow but what did he care, I wasn't one of his models), open my legs and reach between them, and I could feel his eyes smile smugly at finding that familiar secret stash of melting-down Turkish Delight, and I could feel his eyes position themselves so expertly and then just push, push right in because he knew that's the way I like it, and I could feel his eyes close as I cried out and then went completely silent until right at the end, when I came, with a sequence of sobbing and screaming that I am told is truly shocking to behold. ('Did you *really* come?' he asked me the first time we'd slept together. I gasped and slapped his face. He smiled, caught my hand and kissed it: 'I'm sorry, Nicole, but you were just so brilliant! I didn't think girls came that big outside of skin flicks.') Yes, reader, his eyes did all this. And people think ventriloquists have something just because they can throw their voices!

I fought my way groggily through my mash scenario and got in there before Liza had a chance to answer. 'It's sort of open-ended, Matt. Sort of unstructured. Like . . . something by Commes des Garçons.'

He looked hard at me. It was a combination of two things, and I recognised them because I so often felt them right back for him. Lust, and an incredible degree of irritation. 'Nicole, can you come into the bathroom for a moment? Angel,' he added as an afterthought. Then he smiled at Liza. 'Shut your eyes a minute, Mrs S, will you? Just while I get some clothes on.'

'Call me Liza.' She screwed up her eyes tight, like a little girl, wicked. 'I seen it all before, anyway.'

In the case of my husband's dick, you and everyone else, I thought grimly as I trudged to the bathroom. Now I know I keep referring to Matthew's infidelity, but I don't *believe* it yet, really, as such. For a start, he *knows* he's not going to have sex more brilliant than he has with me. And also I sort of feel that as long as I can keep making jokes about it to myself, it can't really be happening. Because then I'd *know*, and the jokes would have to stop. Because they'd hurt too much. But while they don't hurt, he can't really be doing it. Yes, I know I'm sad.

He was at my side. 'Why do we have to go into the bathroom?' I hissed.

'Because I'm afraid I'll fall down the pan and drown by myself, aren't I?' he snapped. He gave me a shove, which was a major moisture producer on my part, I'm afraid. Against my better judgement some mild form of physical violence makes me do a very good imitation of Niagara Falls, and there's not a damn thing I can do about it. 'Just do it!'

We went into the bathroom and he locked the door. He stood against it, looking at me. Then he took out some cigarettes and offered me one. He lit it. His hand trembled. Big hands, very sexy. Though I'd always thought he was great-looking, I'd never realised he was sexy until I looked at his hands closely.

I was living with this unnaturally handsome black journalist when I met Matt. Matt had been at Cambridge with him, and Remi thought Matt was a real bimbo for becoming a photographer. Talk about big, this Remi was huge. But his party-sized penis was to be his downfall so far as I was concerned. Look at it from his angle: he was a gorgeous, brilliant black hack with a cock that looked like a truncheon, and had the same consistency most of the time too. Matt Miller, his old adoring sidekick, was a skinny, girlish white boy in a certifiably mindless profession. Naturally Remi didn't think twice about letting his girlfriend stay up late talking to the guy while he got an early night because he had to go to Malawi for his newspaper next morning.

So Matt and I were talking when suddenly he does this thing. He doesn't leap on me, or snog me. He extends his hand to me, almost shyly, like a girl. I look at his pretty face, with the wide eyes and the pouty mouth – it's a teen idol's face, definitely, the sort of face that very young girls, scared of sex, would love – and the only jarring note this very dark stubble coming through even though his hair is dark blond and his skin is fair, and it really is like a kick in the stomach to realise how hot I am for this boy that Remi and I imitate and make fun of when he's not there: his luvviness, his mindless job, his middle-classness (Remi's family used to run a good-sized piece of Ghana or somewhere, but *he's black so it doesn't count*). The contrast between his girlishness and his masculinity is beautiful to me, and I look down at his hand holding mine, to play for time.

I unclasp my hand and examine his, stretching out the fingers. I see for the first time how big his hand is, and in a pornographic poster second I see the whole hand driving right into me, up to the wrist, and I can hear my own short, shocked scream, then silence.

I look up at him and smile, and my voice trembles when I speak: 'What lovely hands you have, Matt. Really middle-class hands. You can tell you've never done a day's real work in your life.'

He lifts the other hand and slaps me briefly and matter-of-factly across the face with it. 'Shut up.' Then he lifts the first hand to my mouth. 'Kiss it.'

I look at him, and I'm gone from then on. I turn the palm of his hand to my mouth, and I cover it with kisses. It's like I'm trying to eat it. I look at him, and he's smiling, but it's not what smiles are meant to be for. Maybe he's heard Remi and me laughing at him or maybe he just guessed. Whatever, he's not as dumb as we thought and he's come for his revenge.

I was so completely aroused then, when he pulled his hand away I was gasping for breath like an asthmatic. I would have done anything, *and I do mean anything*. But he stood up and smiled and said: 'Tell Remi I had a great time.' And he just left. I had to masturbate six times that night before I could get to sleep, and then only for three hours. I couldn't even lift a pencil the next day. I was ruined, in more ways than one.

Anyway, we went on like this for months. Old Tom Eliot said that people measured out their wasted lives in coffee spoons; I measured out mine in a few hundred gallons of arousal juice whipped up almost off-handedly by Matt Miller over a thousand and one (actually around a dozen, but it seemed more) nights of temptation and frustration. Suddenly, without my even seeing it, I had been pitched into one of those parasexual relationships I had always feared and loathed: the I-wouldn't-want-to-sleep-with-anyone-who'd-want-to-sleep-with-me type – a sophisticated variation of what we used to play at Mixed Infants, the game of Kiss-Chase. Which is: boy chases girl, catches girl, kisses girl – boy runs off. I didn't see the fucking point of it at six, quite frankly, and I certainly don't see it now.

'*Why* run off?' I'd wail at Zoë, who was similarly perplexed. 'If they like you, why can't they kiss you and *stay*?'

'They're *programmed*,' she'd say.

'What are they, *robots*?'

'Hey, keeed – you only just *noticed*?'

I was made brutally aware that, if I wanted Matt, the one thing that would win him would be pretending not to want him. For someone like me, candid to the point of insanity, this counted as some sort of sensory deprivation. I was like an alcoholic, staring at the telephone until I salivated – *one day at a time*. Finally I beat my own record and I called up Zoë to crow.

'Hey, Zo – guess how long I didn't call Matt for?'

'How long?'

'Two days!'

She hung up. I called back.

'But to be honest, on one of them, my phone was out of order.'

I finally went to Cornwall to do some drawing, and stayed in this beautiful hotel in Penzance run by this gorgeous Sixties model. There were no phones in the rooms – *no phones*! There was one phone in the office, and I was damned if I was going to chase any man while Jean Shrimpton looked on pityingly. Treat 'em mean and keep 'em keen, girl – like I did with Terry Stamp! I've got *some* pride.

I got back to London just in time to give Remi a farewell suck job before he rushed off to some trouble-spot or other. Trouble-spot! It was in his own back yard, so to speak. I was lying on the bed, feeling at once used and neglected, when the phone rang.

'Hello?'

'It's Matt. Where the fuck have you been?'

'What's it to you?'

'Shut the fuck up. Is Remi there?'

'He's just gone to South America.'

'I'm coming over.'

I lay there, waiting. I felt that if I jumped up and brushed my teeth and put make-up on, he wouldn't come after all. Yet if I lay there all crusty and nasty he'd come through with it at last. Sure enough, ten minutes later there was a ring at the doorbell.

I stared at him stupidly. He hustled me impatiently inside, pushed me against the door and kissed me.

'Your mouth tastes disgusting.'

'I'm sorr –'

He made an impatient sound and manhandled me into the bedroom, pushed me on to the bed.

'Pull the shade!' I bleated.

'Oh, for –' He pulled the shade and threw himself on top of me. Instantly the poison of our bitter courtship seemed to evaporate as our clothes came off and I discovered how sweet he was to touch and to taste, especially to taste. He smiled as he fucked me, straight into my eyes (unfortunate construction of sentence there, but anyway) and kissed my forehead, murmuring, 'Oh, Nicky, Nicky!' Oddly, he never called me Nicky again; this either means nothing, or it means A Lot. And you don't want to even think about it.

When I finally came, screaming the place down, I was half aware of Matt staring at me with some bemusement and not a little self-love: Did *I* do that? No, I wanted to say, *I* did. But I couldn't be sure, could I, who'd really done it – and he looked so pleased with himself. I felt damn good – it had worked – that was the main thing.

When I calmed down he raised himself on his elbows and looked down into my face. 'Your make-up's a mess, and you look like a complete whore after a hard nightshift,' he said. But – I don't know – there was more affection in those rather unkind words than there had been in the whole past few months of weasel words: 'You know *I really, really* like you.' 'I value you too much as a friend to become your lover.' 'You're so *warm*, Nicole. Put down that pencil and kiss me.' 'No, no, this is all wrong! Remi's my friend. My *friend*!' This last one spoken with his groin grinding against mine, both big hands trying to physically remove by the famous 'twist-off' method my breasts from my upper body, and his tongue doing some sort of dental inspection of my back teeth.

So that's when he said, 'Did you *really* come?' and I slapped him. But as he said later, in a rare moment of wisdom (because he *is* a bimbo, there's no two ways about it): 'Nicole, you've never hit me because you're angry. You've only ever hit me when you wanted me to hit you. So in future why not just say so, and cut out the middle man, so to speak.' Like I'm going to say, 'Hit me!' To *him*, who hasn't even read *The Female Eunuch*!

So where was I? Right, we're locked in the lavatory, smoking like teenage fiends. He's glaring at me re Gran, but there's something else there too. It's a sort of anger-lust, which is great if you've got three hours with just the two of you locked in an ironmonger's shop but not so hot in a confined space with your gran waiting for her Horlicks outside.

He pointed at the toilet. 'Sit.'

I sat down and almost fell into it.

'Oh, for Pete's sake, Nicole!' He hauled me up and put the lid down.

'Well, I didn't know, did I?' Despite myself I was already making insinuations. At my own husband! This is surely the height of decadence. 'You might have wanted me to . . . do something.'

He smouldered at me; I swear, Matt can actually smoulder. 'Don't start. Don't think you can use sex to get out of trouble, like you always do.'

'Ah, but Matt, that's a bit smarter than using sex to get *into* trouble, isn't it?'

'Just shut it, will you? OK.' He inclined his head towards the loft. 'What's all this in aid of?'

I squirmed. 'All what?'

'The Granny From Hell out there.' He flicked his butt through the window, not easy if you're not a contortionist. 'The one I almost had it off with five minutes ago.'

'Oh.' I looked at his feet. If hands are one of the sexiest things about people, feet are one – or two – of the worst. What's a sexy foot look like? You can see why some people go for amputees when you look closely at a foot. 'Well, my mother – my parents – were going to have her put in a Home. Isn't that amazing?'

'How so?' he pouted. He's my age, you'd think he was too old to pout – but somehow, Matt seems to keep looking *younger*. That's how you know you're really getting old – not when the policemen start to look young, but when your husband does. 'Both of *my* grandmothers are in Homes, as you so commonly call them. They're dead happy, too. All those old biddies to push around.'

'Dead happy, or just *dead*?' I'm determined to dig my feet in over this one; they may be ugly, but they've got to be useful for something. 'You don't *know* my Gran, Matthew. She's not like ordinary old people. One of those . . . places would drive her mad.'

'Instead of which she's going to stay here and drive you mad instead.'

'It's not going to *be* like that, Matt.' I thought about it. 'What do you mean, "you"?'

'Damn right it's not going to be like that for me, is what I mean. I'm off to Martinique next week – got it in Mauritius, Fabio double-booked. But I don't fancy your chances much.' He squinted at me. He's the only man I've ever seen who looks sexy squinting. 'And what about when I *am* here? What about when we want to – you know?'

'Fuck.' I said it slowly and lubriciously. I saw his tongue move inside his mouth, and other stuff move besides. I felt tired, and ready to go all night long. 'Well I . . . there's those screens around her bed. And the Japanese manage somehow.'

'Nicole.' He gestured for me to stand up. He took my seat and pulled me on to his knees. 'Japanese women don't scream the place down, darling, every time they get shafted. They imitate twittering morning birdsong.'

'How do you know?' I squirmed jealously. He held me tight.

'Common knowledge.'

'Yeah. In your case, *very* common.'

He smiled at me, and I could tell he still liked me, even though I was his wife. Then he said, 'Oh, baby . . .' and his pretty pink teenage idol mouth opened as it came towards me and I knew I was about to fall in.

I held back. 'How was the shoot?'

'Great. Great.' His hands moved over my back under my T-shirt, impatiently, like someone looking for their place in a book, and finally, like he hadn't been looking for them, he got hold of my breasts.

'And how was that new girl?' I knew I was behaving just like a woman, when all I wanted to do was take it like a man. 'The seventeen-year-old? Siobhan Thing?'

'Oh, great, great.' My T-shirt was around my neck by now and Matthew had found his late lunch. He never could stand aeroplane food. 'She's a very intelligent young woman, actually. She was reading Donna Tartt –' He went back to his oral gratification.

I gasped. But I wasn't ready to give up the ghost. 'How very appropriate.'

He stopped sucking, and scowled at me. '*And* Martin Amis.'

'No doubt you helped her through the extensive

passages on white lacy underwear, and the removal of such.'

We were glaring at each other like two children facing off over a prize at Pass the Parcel, quite appropriate from what I know of Siobhan Thing. I ask you. Only the institution of marriage makes it possible for a woman to have a full-on fight with a man while her nipples are dripping with his saliva. I guess it's progress of a type, but really.

He looked at my face, then my talent, and then he laughed. He pushed his face right into my chest. 'Oh, just can it, Nic!' He laughed up at me. *No*, he was *pretty*, oh *no*. 'Come on, see sense – youth and purity just don't do it for me. Never have done.' He looked me full in the eye, got this whole bunch of spit into his mouth and targeted it right to my heart. I gasped. 'Well, if they did, I wouldn't be with you, would I? Come on, darlin' – just a quick one.'

That did it. I took his head in my hands and brought my mouth down on his. We were both open. It was like if we'd got any more open our faces would have split. You've seen those sea anemones with their sucker stuff: that's what our mouths were like. I couldn't believe we were married. I couldn't believe how much he irritated me. I couldn't believe how fast I came, with his fist in my mouth, with his knife in my heart.

Chapter **Six**

'It was lucky I *did* come – excuse my French, doctor – so quick because he hadn't stopped throbbing before Liza was banging on the door yelling for her Horlicks – of course, the name of the beverage alone just cracked Matt up. Why couldn't it have been Ovaltine? He just lay there on the bathroom floor, laughing himself stupid; that was all I needed –'

'You love him very much, don't you?' said Usha softly. I'm not *paying* her an arm, a leg and half my pubic hair for *that* piece of oriental wisdom, am I?

I scowled for a moment, then I couldn't help but laugh. 'Oh, Usha, he said *such* a funny thing that night, too! He'd met this guy who said my drawing was flashy and shallow, and guess what Matt said to him? He said: "*Heyyy* – don't diss my "ho'."'

She just stared back at me, poker-faced.

'It's like – *you* know – a *black* thing,' I explained helpfully. Then I felt uncomfortable. Was this racist? But then, did Asians really think of themselves as blacks? Only if they were working overtime at being professional ethnics, I decided.

She shrugged; Memsahib Muck. Then she frowned.

'One thing, Nicola, I don't understand. I felt before that your marriage to Matthew was in some way finished, in essence if not in fact. Now it seems that you're on some sort of second honeymoon. Can you clarify this?'

Snoop, snoop, snoop. *Why* does she think I want to think about this? 'Well, doctor . . .'

'Usha.'

'Usha. Well, Usha . . . I blush to admit this, but it's a sex thing. I've been with this – this *person*, if you like, for five years. I haven't slept with anyone else during that whole time, except in my dreams. Against my will. I can honestly say that I don't know one other couple in our set who've stayed together that long, even when they *were* putting it about. Basically, I suppose, our relationship is a poke in the eye to all those marriage-guidance experts who say that for a marriage to succeed the couple have to have background and interests and temperament in common. We don't have anything in common except sex.'

'How so?' She looked dead interested now. It's great being a shrink. Think about it. Six separate soap operas a day.

'Well, he's incredibly middle class. His accent. I'm not being chippy here. I've got this really, really upper-class girlfriend. I love listening to her talk. It's like hearing history, like hearing those old working-class voices from the war. But Matthew . . . I don't know. There's a certain sort of young male middle-class voice which just sounds like a *smirk*. That's what he's got. Even when he thinks he's being thoughtful and solemn and he tries to talk about politics. I've never heard anyone talk seriously about torture in Latin America, like he used to do with Remi, and just sound as though he was *smirking*. It's not just me; Remi was just the opposite of me, he was black as the ace of spades and some sort of aristo. But he grabbed me by the shoulders when I mentioned it one night, and laughed like crazy, and kissed me and said I was *absolutely right*! *Matt couldn't stop smirking!* After that, Remi and I used to do this really mean thing. If some terrible atrocity came on the news, we'd see who could be the first to do Matt talking about it.' I giggled nostalgically, then saw the look on her face. She was right: it was a really ugly thing to do. And not because of poor little Matt, but because of the atrocity. I tried to limbo under her deadly logic. 'It was a long time ago,' I added weakly, 'and anyway, Remi was *African* . . .'

'Good for bloody Remi,' she snapped. I gaped at her, and she coloured up again. She isn't half attractive when she blushes. 'Go on. Why else are you incompatible?'

'Oh, Usha! He thinks photography is *art*.' I stared boldly at her; I wasn't even going to *justify* this one. 'And our temperaments. Matt thinks that problems are God's way of telling us to go to another hemisphere for a spell. *I* think problems are there to be made a purée of: mashed up, destroyed. Matt says I'm very combative, a control freak actually,' I said, trying to sound ashamed of myself. Quite frankly, this is one of the things, along with my big green eyes, that I like most about myself.

'But still, you get along together. Where other, more obviously suited couples, fail . . .'

'Yes. I suppose so. But oh, doctor, oh Usha, I really

don't think I've ever been so purely *irritated* by a human being in my life . . .'

'Go on.' What a life! I'm in the wrong racket.

'Well, I've noticed this thing about Matt. And not just Matt, bless him, but his friends. About a certain sort of modern man. The sort of man who thinks he's like quite a few evolutionary steps up from your Essex Man or your lager lout. Do you know what I mean?'

Usha smiled and she used her shrub catalogue – she's quite shameless about showing it to me now, I'm obviously not worth putting up a pretence for – like a fan, cooling herself with it and then twinkling – you! My brown-eyed girl! – over the top at me. 'Oh, Nicola! Surely you know by now that I am an Asian virgin, and have very little experience, if any, of the male animal?'

'Well, this sort of man (Matthew) thinks he's really superior to the sort of slob who says yucky macho things. But *they* say them too. *They* talk about shagging and getting their end away. About quick ones. They call you "darlin' " and "luv" and "babe". But they say stuff like "Let me shag you stupid" with, like, quotation marks around it.' I made the air-quotes gesture myself, feeling really dumb. 'So it's meant to be OK. Do you understand?'

Usha nodded. 'Through you, Nicola, I feel I understand.' Dig that! I'm not a racist, but I saw how it would seem to my parents. I came all this way – to act as a translator, making one lot of white people understandable to an ethnic, whom I was actually *paying* for the privilege! I tried to get past it, like a modern girl would.

'But when they say things like that, with the quotes

around it, it makes me think of that fat comedian actor who's always turning up to things in a stretch limo. And when his Green friends call him on it, he goes, "Oh, it's an *ironic* limousine." ' I sat up and pawed the air excitedly at Dr Alibhai. 'But that doesn't mean that this ironic car gives off any less pollution, does it? No, it doesn't! Any less than an ironic sexual advance makes it any less insulting to the person it's directed at.' I was full of it now. 'Isn't irony just a smart excuse for saying dumb things?'

'Are you saying, Nicola, that you didn't want to have sexual intercourse with Matthew?' Talking of dumb things! Thanks a lot, Usha.

I'm paying her too much to lie to her: ''Course I do.'

'And how is Matthew taking to your grandmother?'

'Well, since you ask, he was only back for three days between jobs. And he slept through most of those. When he was there, that is. When he wasn't over at his "studio" – accent on the S.T.U.D. "Developing", he calls it. Developing Siobhan Thing's thigh muscles, no doubt.'

'And have you told Matthew of these fears, Nicola?'

I laughed – hollowly, I hope. 'Sure I've told him. Usually in Anglo-Saxon words of one syllable. Or less. Usually at a decibel count that's brought the wrath of the neighbours down on me more than once.' I considered, then confessed. 'And I'm talking about neighbours as far as four doors down.'

Hey, old Usha, she's like some Bob Dylan dream woman; she knows too much to argue or to judge. Or rather, she's being *paid* too much to do either. 'And what does Matthew have to say with reference to his contribution to these disagreements?'

'The usual crap.' I was beyond caring now. Because I cared so much. It's like being left-wing or right-wing, according to some people; eventually they meet up. Personally, I've never seen this. 'That Siobhan Thing's really nice, and that I'm being "negative". That's Matt's answer to everything. He actually said once that I was so negative it was a wonder that photographs didn't pop out of my ears every time I put chemicals up my nose.' I stopped, thinking how to phrase it so that Usha wouldn't get on my case straight away. 'He even says that me having Gran to live with me is negative.'

'Really?' She really was pretty nice. 'Why on earth would he say that?'

I took a deep breath and dived into the deep end. 'Because he says I'm only doing it to spite my mum.'

'And are you?' she says, smart as paint.

'Whoah!' I couldn't believe it! 'Hang about! Whose side are you on?'

'Come, come, Nicola.' Soothingly, like a lie. 'It's not a question of sides . . .'

'Everything's a question of sides,' I said stubbornly. 'Including birth, death and taxes. The only thing that's not a question of sides is a circle.' I thought about it. 'And even they can be vicious, come to think about it.'

Dr Alibhai played with her papers. Like all women, she's been banjaxed by Matthew, even in his absence. Treacherous bitch. But hey, I don't blame her. That's the way men are. Like women used to be. *Honeytraps. Poison. Bad medicine.* They know they're useless, just like women used to be, so they've made themselves fatal. Scratch a man and I'll show you Mata Hari: a spy, a saboteur, especially of his own, most precious relationship. Sugar pie, honeybunch, you know that I love you – Lord, I can't help myself!

'So Matthew is being utterly mistaken when he says these things, about your mother and your grandmother . . .'

'Too bloody right he is!' What am I, a golden retriever in the land of the blind? 'Because you see, doctor, unlike everyone else in this phoney, self-adoring clan my gran somehow managed to spawn, in fact in this phoney, self-adoring *world*, *I'm* the only living breathing human being who actually seems to care whether or not she's having a *good time* . . .'

I followed the white talcum-powder footsteps across the shining black tiles of the bathroom floor to the doorway, and then all across the long expanse of the loft's redwood floor. They criss-crossed and zigzagged, and eventually they led to Liza in her nightdress at the big glass wall.

Ten o'clock, and she's not dressed. This is a way big thing with a geriatric. You and I might not be dressed at ten o'clock easily, for no reason; or because we'd been working, because we'd been fucking, because we'd been lying in bed reading Proust. (Or more likely Terence Kilmartin. Think about it.) But for Liza, believe me, it's a way big thing.

I walked up behind her, and tried to see what she saw. Admittedly the 'hood looked pretty dull and deserted this time on a Tuesday, four floors down. The river looked like someone who'd stayed too long at a party, and was now, next morning, trying to make himself useful to no avail. If I am to be honest, and what else would I be with you, what Liza saw before her now was indeed a very far cry from what she once saw from her window in Victory Street.

'Gran?' She turned and looked at me, somewhat blank. 'If you could just use a little less talc on your feet?' I tried loathsomely to bring a humorous note to the cautioning. 'This place looks as though a ghost has been giving ballroom dancing lessons here!'

She turned back to the view. I went and sat down at my drawing board, starting to sharpen certain of my pencils.

'Why dissn't thee 'ave a budgie?'

There. It had to happen. Still, I feel chilled by determinism. 'You what?'

'A budgie.' She's looking at me now, I know, loving this. 'Why 'asn't thee got one?'

It's a swine, this one. No answer to it, really. I start counting, and drawing. I speak, after a fashion. And after wanting to pull her head off.

'I don't really have time to get into all that budgie/pet/whatever thing right now, Gran. Not at this platform level of my life.'

She snorts. The *lungs* on this woman! She's like a walking commercial for exploiting child labour. 'Whass mean, no time? You'm 'ome all day! 'Ow much time d'you need to stick some budgie seed and some water in two little dishes? And a bit of millet through the bars! And to slide a sheet of newspaper under the poor little bugger?'

I put down my pencils and thought about it, logically. I didn't want to dismiss her ravings out of hand. 'I find it extremely hard to believe that these meagre rations are all that a mature budgerigar requires, Gran. For instance, we know now that even plants – which are non-sentient beings, a bit like my husband – flourish and bloom when talked to and generally taken an interest in. So really, Gran – think how much truer that must be of a budgie!'

She thought – as best she could, one supposes. Then she spoke: 'Wouldn't kill you to pass the time of day with it, would it? You'm 'ere all day, sitting on your jacksy –'

'Hardly,' I said (coldly). 'When I am here, I am working. Unlike most lucky people, I cannot knock off blithely at five o'clock and forget about everything. My work is actually pretty much my life.' I had a think. 'And then there are the lunches. With clients. If the commission is especially complex, these may last up to four hours.'

She's sneering, more authentically than I ever managed, even at fifteen. 'Diddums. What a life.'

'So you see, Gran, a budgie would be rather muddying the water, as it were.'

'Not if you changed it every day.'

By now I knew for sure that the old devil was really trying to wind me up. I turned and narrowed my eyes at her; she widened hers at me. I suddenly thought how depressingly like a marriage – *my* marriage, to make it even more depressing – this one supposedly perfect relationship of my life had become in the space of two weeks. If we'd been asked to write down our hobbies, and we'd been honest about it, I personally don't see how we could have avoided writing, 'Annoying and generally obstructing the person I love more than anyone else in all the world.' I shuddered to think how tiny-minded these persecutions had become when things started to go wrong with Matt, which was approximately after three months, entirely spent in bed.

Matt, in a fit of uncharacteristic restraint, as soon as we decided to get spliced decreed that there should be some sex thing we didn't do until our wedding night. What was it? Right, fight fans – sodomy. Logically, much taken with the shock of the new, this meant Matt fancied a full three months of sodomy after our marriage. This meant that I couldn't sit down for three months, let alone pick a pencil up. This meant, I've always believed, that my career in the wonderful world of commercial art took a nosedive here from which it never fully recovered. And I know it's crazy, but a part of me really does believe that Matt *planned it that way*! He knew he couldn't keep me under his thumb by force or argument – ah, but *sex*. Sodomy was the secret weapon with which he utterly buggered up my career.

And he's not a gentleman; I'll tell you that much. He may be middle class, but he's certainly not a gentleman. When I complained about not being able to sit down, and thus not being able to draw, he said to me: 'Don't give me that, sweetheart. You were *begging* for it.'

What do you say to an aspersion like that? In my case, displaying an honesty this man did not quite deserve, I said: 'How *dare* you refer to those occasions! And as I remember there were only five of them. Possibly six. But certainly no more than ten.'

Matt laughed, quite hilariously for some reason, and then he put his arms around me: 'Nicole, you're too good for me. You're such a good girl.'

Too right. But his good girl soon went bad. I blush

to recall the dozen tiny little things I'd do in a single day to make his life slightly less pleasant than it otherwise would have been. If I knew there was something he really, really wanted to catch on the television or radio – he had a rotten memory, like all unmemorable people – I'd hold my breath in the ten minutes leading up to the time it was due to go out. When I realised that he'd forgotten, and I could have made his life just that millimetre bit nicer by reminding him of it, I felt a thrill that was almost sexual; like shoplifting. Then, here's what I'd do – I'm shameless in front of you, I know, but if not now then when? – the minute before it ended I'd smite my forehead theatrically and groan. 'Ohhh . . .'

'What's wrong, babe?'

'That documentary about Cartier-Bresson you wanted to see! . . . Quick, turn it on, it might not be over yet!'

Invariably, he'd see the credits. He has a child's face, which shows his emotions. Especially disappointment. Ha, ha, ha.

I'll tell you a thing about marriage, shall I? When it goes wrong, you become less than human. You become a child. A wicked fairy. A saboteur. A poltergeist. This other thing I did was break stuff of his. Stuff I knew he really liked. 'Accidentally'. Did I feel guilty? Not at the time. You sort of see a red mist and then it's 'I don't know what came over me, Your Honour.' Because, put yourself in my place, he'd broken stuff of mine that I really liked, accidentally or not. Yeah, it was called my *marriage*.

How did he break your marriage, Nicola, you may ask, when you admit yourself that his adultery is entirely unproven? Well, I'll tell you how. By conveniently fixing it so that he had a job which just happened to *demand* that he spend most of his waking hours in the company of physically perfect seventeen-year-olds. He's a bloody photographer, isn't he? He could easily be doing atrocities, or old guys on the scrapheap in Nebraska. But oh no! It's got to be Siobhan Thing, she of the seventeen summers and as many IQ points, starkers in Sri Lanka.

'I *told* you the guy was a bimbo,' Remi says triumphantly when I phone him at his paper to moan. 'You *would* go off with him, though, wouldn't you? The minute my back was turned. And I was being *shot* at.'

'You were never being shot at!'

'I was too! While you were letting my so-called best friend come in your face, no doubt . . .'

'Oh, Remi . . . I'm sorry. I didn't mean it to happen.'

'Hey, don't sweat it, bitch.' Remi goes into dude mode. 'I can get fifty blondes like you before breakfast.' He's himself again when he says, 'You want to go out for a drink? Just as friends?'

'Thanks, Remi . . . I'd better not.'

'OK. Hey, Nicole –'

'What?'

'Don't trust Whitey.'

Hah! Don't worry, Remi, I don't! I *am* a spy in the House of Love, or rather the Loft of Lust in our case, and I am as adept at decoding diary entries and sniffing out credit-card receipts as any woman with a definite adultery sighting and a case on its way to court. The only trouble is what Matthew does for a living; any other woman who found her husband was planning to see Manda on Monday, Tara on Tuesday, Wanda on Wednesday and so on would have the bastard bang to rights. But as he says, it's his *job*.

As for the credit-card receipts, that's another dead loss. Swimsuits, G-strings, lip gloss, even Tampax; it's pretty damn easy to believe, having met quite a few of them, that these dipsticks really don't remember to take their *money*, yes, that *crinkly* stuff, out with them in their little pink patent purses just big enough to hold a mirror and a bottle of Murine – and as for remembering you're just about to go on the rag in a big way, *forget it*! As Matthew has pointed out (*repeatedly*) these girls are *children trapped in the bodies of women* in many ways (listen to the way men always say that; it starts out all sympathetic and shrink-y, but by the time they get to the syllable 'bod' they're salivating), and so the stylists and photographers have to be brother, mother and –

'Lover?' I invariably snarl. 'Well, it *almost* rhymes.'

'I was going to say "cashpoint",' Matthew will snarl back. 'You paranoid *bitch*.'

Quite a lot like the home life of our own dear future king, no? I mean, I really, really *felt* for Diana. Her husband had a *filet mignon* at home, but he just couldn't resist going out for a bit of scrag end, could he? Well, I think you'll agree that my so-called 'paranoia' is more than justified when you consider that *I'm* the bit of scrag end, *and* I'm at home. Talk about the worst of both worlds. (I'm deviating here for a minute, but I've got this brilliant story that absolutely sums up how profoundly *stupid* Siobhan Thing is. Get this; her real name's 'Bridget' – but she changed it, because she thought 'Bridget' was 'too Irish'! 'What the Sam Hill does she believe the ethnic origin of the name "Siobhan" is?' I demanded of Matthew as he fiddled with his zoom lens. At least he had the decency to look abashed. 'Thai.')

And now, for that finishing touch that makes a woman absolutely irresistible to a man, I'm a bit of scrag end at home with an *en suite* grandmother. Oh yeah, I've got all mod cons, me, everything a girl needs to line a right little love shack. Siobhan's got a jacuzzi in her bathroom; I've got a commode in mine. Her spotless bathroom shelves are lined with the latest tempting bath goodies from Shiseido; mine are lined with Deep Heat and corn plasters. Her fridge whispers 'Come and get me, big boy!' when opened in post-fuck grazing mode, showing champagne and cherries in erotic metaphor run riot; *my* fridge croaks, 'Piss off! Shut that door! Me Guinness is going off!' Where there's not Guinness, there's meat, everywhere; meat may or may not be murder, but it sure looks like shit in a fridge. 'Meat' is an end in itself to my Gran; whether it's pig, cow, lamb or Spam is beside the point. Receiving a sandwich, all she'll ask is, 'Is it meat?' Given pasta, she'll ask, 'Where's the meat?' As someone who's pretty much a strict vegetarian except when she's drunk, depressed or there's nothing in the fridge *but* meat (which come to think of it covers ninety-nine per cent of all known situations these days) this is pretty much a karmic no-go area for me.

Siobhan's living space is a modish module of light and airiness, blameless shameless shiny surfaces reflecting each other endlessly. Even messy, it looks charming; even her debris has style. Blue bottles and glasses, half full – never half empty, remember, because

Siobhan, unlike *moi*, the moaning wife, is *positive* – positively *glow*, unlike mere mortals' morning-after washing-up, in the early sun. (The sun always shines on Siobhan. It has done for so long that she's come to consider it her own personal spotlight. Galileo had it all wrong, see; the sun revolves around Siobhan.) As well they might, with the memory of having Siobhan's mouth all over them. In fact, if you're a male aged between eighteen and eighty, resident in the Greater London area, then you'll probably know *exactly* how they feel. It's a place to *play*, Siobhan's flat; as befits her extreme youth, it's practically a playpen. It's a place where a man in a high-stress, cut-throat job (i.e. smearing Vaseline on camera lenses so the hairs growing out of Siobhan's nipples won't show so much; sorry, I don't mean to be a bitch. I really, really *like* women. Especially ones living in Ecuador that my husband's never met) can kick off his Timberlands, put his feet up and get a quite adequate blow job while enjoying the first Malibu and Coke of the evening. (I always imagine Siobhan drinking Malibu. I don't know why.) In a while, after she's run to the bathroom and spat it out, rinsed with Plax, brushed her teeth, flossed, Water-Pikked, rinsed with Listerine and put her lipstick on (these models are dead neurotic about sex. Totally asexual. Only do it to be accommodating. Everyone knows that. Please God), they'll feed each other fancy little finger foods from the fridge (let's hope Mr Man washes his mitts first, or everything's going to taste of tuna. Possibly even pilchard) and wash it down with a saucy Sauternes.

(Matthew and I had this game, years ago. When we were in love. What emotion does food taste like?

'Salt and vinegar crisps taste like . . . regret,' I said.

He thought awhile. Very few men look pretty when they think. He did. 'Pear drops . . . taste like sex with a pervert.'

I shove him: 'Sex with a pervert isn't an emotion!'

He shoves me back: 'Depends who the pervert is, dunnit?' He grabs my chin and kisses my mouth hard, before pulling back and squinting into my eyes. He touches his own cheek. 'This face is leaving town first thing tomorrow. *Be on it.*')

When they've stuffed and swilled themselves stupid, they'll do something fun and young, Siobhan and Mr X. They'll probably play a board game, which is a really whacky and fash thing to do right now. Let's see – what board game would they play? How about Risk, since Mr X is married, and to an extremely *negative* woman at that, who's quite likely to cut the crotch out of his suits with him in them if she ever gets solid proof that he's been slipping it to the sort of girl who believes that 'Siobhan' is a name you often hear echoing across the beach at Phuket.

Monopoly, perhaps. You can't beat the classics. Surprise, surprise, Siobhan, you've won a beauty contest! Collect ten snogs from each player, pass Go, grab two hundred pounds. Buy Mayfair and Park Lane and bankrupt me without even trying. Go on – you've had the best, now take the rest! Cluedo's always a good one: all those cute dinky weapons. Here is the gun I'd shoot her with; the knife I'd stab her with; the candlestick I'd bash her brains (hah!) in with and the lead piping I'd stick up the fundament of her still-warm young body. And here is the rope I'd hang myself with, after writing the note: MATT. THIS IS ALL

YOUR FAULT. BUT DON'T BLAME YOURSELF. BE HAPPY. LOVE, NICOLE (YOUR WIFE).

('Who did it, do you think, Nic?' 'Miss Thing, in Mauritius, with the photographer.')

Maybe they're playing Perudo. Hey, it's all about how well you can cheat and lie; this bout's going to be a long one, isn't it? These are the grandmasters of the game, after all. It just might be Trivial Pursuit; but Siobhan will pout, sulk and finally upset the board when she can't come up with the capital of England.

No, it's got to be Twister. No stressful questions to distress Siobhan. No need for skill, thought or concentration. The only thing you need for Twister is a supple seventeen-year-old body and a complete lack of modesty. And someone else's husband. All these being present and correct, Twister is a great excuse to get your twat stuck on someone's nose. And sure enough, the dice haven't been cast more than four times before Siobhan and Mr X – who, let's face it, is actually Mr M – fall to the floor and copulate enthusiastically on the innocent Twister sheet.

There are tears in my eyes.

'Nic! NIC!'

I attempt to make a crash landing as I return from Planet Masochistic Fantasy, fuelled by the urgency in Liza's voice. 'Gran?' I start to walk towards her.

She's running now, in her nightie, for the door. 'Quick, Nic! A little tart's been knocked off her bike! All them bleedin' great lorries out there, too!' I catch up with her, and she shakes me by the shoulders. She looks fifteen years younger: she looks, I realise with slow-motion sorrow, the happiest and most alive she has looked since coming here. 'Come on!'

'Gran!' I grab at her. 'You can't just – You don't even know who –'

She pulls away. Nothing's going to stop her now. 'She'm fallen off 'er bike, I told 'ee! You deaf or summat?'

'But you don't even know her!' I yell. Too late; she's out of here. 'Gran!'

I follow, chasing her shadow, choking on her dust.

Chapter **Seven**

I took against that *child*, which is what the fiend was disguised as, from the first moment I saw her.

Picture this: there's a skinny little girl of twelve lying bleeding on the tarmac of a busy London highway. Her undernourished little body, with those heartbreaking Olive Oyl legs pubescent girls often have (that's a nasty word, isn't it? On a par with 'gusset' and 'crust', really; *pube*scent. What do you bet a *man* thought it up? To embarrass young girls, no doubt) seems even frailer because of the size of the merciless juggernauts roaring by. Beside her, and a bit on top of her, is her bike; one of those fuck-you don't-touch-me jobs that working-class families go without Class A drugs for a year for, so that on Christmas morning little Vichyçoise or Tarquin (it's always the families with the least to bequeath in the way of material goods who leave their kids really fancy names, have you noticed? The American inner-city working-class blacks, for instance. All their daughters have names like people sneezing: Kanisha! Tanisha! Shaniqua! Jalisa! Latasha! Aisha! It must be a real scream calling the school register in the morning, especially if the teacher's got a cold to start with) can at last glory in the clean, lean machine of their dreams, take it out for a celebratory spin and break their necks by Boxing Day.

You'd expect to feel sorry for the piteous little creature, wouldn't you? Crushed by the wheels of avarice with a dirty great Euro-lorry bearing down on her. A game little Cockney sparrer who might never sing again. You'd expect that you might feel like making her up into a bundle and holding her against your warm, nurturing body and taking her home where you'd patch up her wounds and feed her hot chocolate and make up a bed on the sofa and turn on CITV while you called her parents. You'd let her go, when they finally arrived, because her place was with them – but you'd shed a tear, silently, in the still of the night, for your little Cockney sparrer who flew away all too soon.

But quite frankly, the moment I set eyes on Michaela, I wanted to push her face in.

'Nic'la!' Liza is shoving at me. 'What biss thee playing at, wench? Thee biss like a tart in a trance!' She stoops down to get closer to the little girl. I note resentfully and probably inappropriately under the circs that old biddies of her age aren't meant to be *able* to stoop. Is it possible that she is an impostor? 'Oi! Can thee move? Put yer arms round me neck. There you go. Now try and stand up. Never mind. Nic'la! Get 'er feet!'

I don't like this 'Nic'la' stuff; guiltily, I think of how Teresa accused me of only calling her 'Mother' when I didn't approve of her. I hesitate, then take the fiend's feet half-heartedly. Between us, we just about half drag, half carry the creature on to the pavement.

It opens its eyes. Its eyes are blue. Like frostbite. 'My bike!' it pipes. It has an unpleasant voice, thug Cockney to the rag and bone. This is the sort of voice that grows up to twist arms.

''Er bike!' Liza parrots, staring at me as though I'm simple. 'Go and get it, then!'

Don't worry about *me*, anyone, will you! Risking life and limb, I and my thighs strike out boldly into Dead Man's Curve and somehow manage to grab the bike, slapping its face when it becomes hysterical. I head back for the shore, pulling it after me. When I get there, what do you know? There's no welcome party for little Nicola. No bunting for the bi-baby who's gone a-hunting and come up with the goods. The sidewalk is bare, there's nobody there. I've been binned. By my own grandmother. My gran.

I take the bike into the building and leave it in the foyer. I bang the lift button with a bad grace. Of *course* it isn't working. Because Liza's forgotten to close the outside grille properly. No, not forgotten, *done it on purpose*. So I'll have to walk up. You think I'm raving. But I know this for a fact because I once caught her opening it when I decided to take the stairs instead. This is one of the ways in which she sabotages my life. *This is her life.*

I start up the stairs, muttering to myself. It turns into a song, a song that was a hit before my mother was born, quite likely. 'I'll build a stairway to paradise, with a new stair every day, I'm going to get there at any price . . .'

I had this friend, Isabella. Isabella was very, very rich. You knew she was rich because she called it 'being quite comfy'. I was often trying to think of a modern riposte to F. Scott Fitz's 'The rich are different from us' in those days; out shopping with Izzy one day, I got it: *The rich are different from us because they never look at price tags.*

Now, this actually isn't true. Not at all. It's only true of extremely hedonistic aristos and a goodly proportion of the nooves. *But that's not the point!* It's such a good line that authenticity is rather the icing on the cake, and we all know by now that icing's not good for you. Best avoided, in fact. Which proves my point.

And that was what I had done. Once again, I'd acted like a real high roller and completely ignored the price I'd have to pay when I went in there and took Liza. I'd done the same when I chucked a prince like Remi for a prat like Matt. I was like an inverted version of those poor buggers who get a bump on the head and completely lose their memories; I mean *everything* in their memories, like they have to ask their wretched, heartbroken wife what her name (the wife's) is literally every other minute. I really seemed to believe that there wasn't going to be a future, there wasn't going to be a bill to settle at the end of the evening, so I really might as well do as I pleased. That was why I never, ever looked at the price tags.

I think it might be to do with the nuclear bomb. But I couldn't swear to it.

The creature was stretched out on my sofa when I finally reached civilisation. Moaning as though she was having a multiple orgasm. Which is a bit sick, in a twelve-year-old. I stood there in the doorway looking at her. I didn't go too close because I didn't want to block the path of Sally Field, who obviously was going to rush in any minute now and present the little beast with the Academy Award for Best Actress. And a dead cert for Best Supporting was obviously Liza Sharp, gazing down upon the malingering little git with a tenderness she'd definitely never shown towards *me*, her own flesh and blood.

It sat up sharpish when it saw me, though. Mid-moan. 'Where's my bike?' it hissed.

'Downstairs.' I walked into the kitchen and poured myself a drink. A hard one, not a soft one. Of course, water's my favourite drink – when all's said and done. And *only* then. Boom boom!

'Bring it up, then!' Its head was practically revolving in a ninety-degree turn, like Linda Blair's in *The Exorcist*. To me, *The Exorcist* proved conclusively that there is demonic possession in this our twentieth-century civilisation. Because why else would Mike Oldfield have made *Tubular Bells*? 'Else someone'll nick it!'

'No one will "nick" it, as you put it.' My pink gin and I went to take a closer look at it. 'It isn't that sort of building.'

'No, but it's that sort of bike,' it comes back, quick as a flash. It makes as if to rise from the sofa. Accent on 'as if'.

Liza lunges at it, pinning it down. It looks well pleased. 'Nic'la, go and get the wench's bike! Before she does 'erself a mischief!'

'But Gran –'

'Just do it, Nic'la! Buggeration – I could jump through you!'

I go out, but I listen at the door.

''Ere we are.' The old black mammy sets down a

tray at the feet of the living deity with the runny nose. 'Tizer suit you?'

'Yeah, I love it!' I hear it guzzling from the glass. *My* glass. 'I never have it at home, though. My mum says it's fattening.'

'So? You'm all skin and bone. Ain't right on a kiddy.' Having served Simon Legree Barbie first, the humble factotum takes her own refreshment. If anything she makes a more obscene noise than the creature. 'D'you want the telly on?'

'Please . . .'

'We got cable,' Liza says smugly. What you mean, *we*, white woman? I have to walk away now, or I wouldn't be able to stop myself from charging in there, wrenching the TV remote from my precious, frail grandmother's hand, giving her a shove that sends her flying straight into the cold comfort of the Amish (or Shaker, or Quaker) chair and turning on the Open University programme (Geology) just to show them who's boss. It's such a *male* thing, isn't it? The pecking order.

So I go down and get the bike. I drag it up the stairs because – yes! – I forgot to close the lift's outer grille. I wheel it in, wheel it right up to the creature without speaking, and stand there looking at her.

She's sucking the chocolate off a Dime bar. Her eyes seem frozen to the TV screen, like a child's tongue to an ice lolly.

'Here it is.'

'Cheers.'

'What's your name?' I bet it's Solange. Or Bianca.

'Michaela.' Its eyes don't flicker. Liza's sitting to one

side of it, looking at it as if it's just laid a golden egg the size of Slough. 'Micci. With two Cs.'

'That doesn't spell "Micky".' I drop the bike, and it plays dead. The fiend looks daggers at me. 'It spells "Missy".'

'No it doesn't.' Her nasty little cold blue eyes seem to be filed to points as they glare at me. 'My best friend's called Jacci. With two Cs. The C is hard.'

'A bit like life,' I mutter, glaring at Gran. Who doesn't notice, of course. Being riveted to the sweet mystery of life scratching itself on the sofa.

But hark! It speaks. 'What biss thee moaning on about?' Liza snaps at me. She then turns to the she-succubus. Her voice goes to mush. 'You 'ungry, Mick?'

Well, lookabye, lookabye! When it talks to Liza, it actually peels its eyes off the screen. And fixes its gaze on Gran as though she was Boyzone in its entirety, proffering engagement rings on bended, bleeding knees. 'I'm ravishing,' says Michaela.

'Hardly,' I whisper viciously to my pink gin.

'My mum wants me to be a supermodel, see.'

'Whass that, when it's at 'ome?' Gran demands. "Ere, Nic – dap down the chippy for us.'

'But, Gran, the cassoulet's almost –'

'Come on, be a pal.' But I'm *not* a pal. I'm your *true love*. 'Get us two cod, two chips, two pickled onions.'

'Can I have a saveloy?' Michaela pipes up.

Don't tempt me, darling! 'You most certainly can,' I say, controlling myself. Muttering like a madwoman, 'So long as I personally can stick it right down your throat.'

'Cheers,' it mouths cheerlessly. Then it bats its meagre eyelashes at Liza. 'Are you her nan?'

'Gran,' I rasp.

'Yes, love.' Liza beams.

'Oh.' The fiend is finally feeling sorry for itself, after a lifetime of triumphalism. 'I don't have a nan of my own.' You won't believe this, but it leaps up and throws its front legs around Liza's middle! 'Will *you* be my nan?'

It's like a car crash. I'm looking, but I don't want to look. The horror, the horror: *Gran's actually hugging her. She's laughing.*

''Course I will!'

'And do you know, Usha, I had to walk out right that minute. Because if I hadn't, and I mean this literally, I would have wailed, "No! She can't! She's *my* gran! *Only* mine!" ' I turn my face towards my pristine princess. 'Isn't that pathetic?'

'Nooo,' she says, very carefully. 'Not . . . pathetic. *Different*. A little unusual, perhaps.' She shifts in her chair. I wonder if her skin sticks to the seat, or whether she's all cool and dry. Look at this, will you? That man has pushed me so far to hell and back, I'm turning into a raving dyke. I'll soon be going to *Helen* and back. 'You're extremely attached to your grandmother – she *is* your family.'

'Well, obviously . . .' Give that girl a lollipop.

'No. No, you misunderstand me,' she flaps excitedly. 'You misunderstand when I say that she is your family. I mean it literally. I don't just mean she is a *member* of your family; I mean that she is in some way all the family you have. Your relationship with your parents is remote and antagonistic, especially with your mother. The same with your husband, with whom sex would seem to be all you have in common.'

'And there's not even too much of that these days,' I moan. 'D'you know what time Bridget the Midget called up the other night? Three a.m. There's a certain sort of person who calls up at three a.m., don't you think, Usha? If twelve's the witching hour, then three's the neurotic-slut-sloshed-on-Malibu-playing-Alanis-Morrisette-records-calling-married-boyfriend hour, isn't it?'

'Now, Nicola,' Dr Beat scolds gently, 'you *know* you don't have any concrete proof . . .'

'No, but if I did, I'd bash them both over the heads with it.'

She laughs, but uneasily. She's scared I'm a nutter. That's a joke, isn't it? She's a shrink – and she's getting all nervous because she thinks I might be mad. Really. Would I be here if I wasn't? 'Yes, but as I was saying . . . in your grandmother, you find the one relation who makes you feel good about yourself.'

'*Used* to, Usha. *Used* to.' I blink away the tears. 'Until that poisonous little bloodsucker came along.'

I'm working at my board on these fashion illustrations for *Elle*. I'm going for a sort of cyber-Erté look, girls with Eton crops and monocles but also nose-rings and Doc Marten's. Gran's gone to her regular soirée at the local launderette, where the local biddies congregate to sip dry Martinis and make sophisticated smalltalk about the state of their bowels. It's really, really working and I'm completely caught up in it when I suddenly realise *I'm not alone*. There would appear to be another human being in the loft. Or rather, Michaela.

She mooches over to me. I put down my pencil and sit back in my chair with my hands folded lethally in my lap. It's a bit childish, I know, this I'm-not-going-to-do-it-while-you're-looking shtick, but Michaela has that effect on me. In fact, I figure I may as well be hung for a sheep as a lamb and actually cover my work up with my hands, like the swots do at school.

She recognises the gesture and smirks in a big way. Like Matthew, whose bastard (in both senses) daughter she could easily be – dark blond hair, fair skin, six o'clock shadow – a smirk seems to be the natural repose of her features. Hey, don't knock it – they've probably got a great future together, old Micci and Matt. After all, she's only five years younger than Siobhan.

She picks up one of my fruity pastilles, one of the very expensive ones, and starts fiddling with it. The dumb cluck obviously thinks it's some sort of eye-shadow. 'Why haven't you got any children?'

I pick up my pencil quickly. I can't live through this without a prop. An Uzi would be favourite, but I can make do with a Rexel Cumberland Derwent Graphic 6B at a pinch. 'Put that down,' I say. She does so, with a bad grace, but picks up an even more expensive oil pastel. 'Because they might turn out like you.' I put the tip of my tongue between my lips as I concentrate on the cyber-Erté girl's crooked elbow. She's got a long, elegant, ebony cigarette holder, out of which hangs the most enormous joint this side of Remi. 'And then I'd have to murder them, wouldn't I, and then I'd get put in jail, and then I wouldn't be able to wash my hair once a day. Had enough?'

She puts down the oil pastel, slightly shocked but not bowed. 'You think you're smart, don't you?' she sneers.

'Damn right.' I sat back and looked at what I'd done with some satisfaction. A fox with a beatbox. I could fancy her myself if she wasn't five inches high. Still, I've made the best of five inches before. As my husband will testify.

'You're not so smart.' Michaela pauses before delivering the killer. '*Nan* says.'

I'm dead cool. '*Gran* says, you mean. *My* gran. *Mrs Sharp* to you.'

'Nan says that if you were as smart as you think you are,' she goes on doggedly, the bitch, 'then your husband would stay home more. Instead of chasing off across the world after some –'

'Why don't you go and play by the river, Michaela?' I enquire sweetly. 'I'll give you a nice push to start you off.'

'You want children, though, don't you?' she carries on. She's like a bloody lawnmower. Get too near to that motormouth when it's full speed ahead and you could lose a few fingers without even trying.

I decide to take the patient approach and wear her down. All she's after is a reaction. If I don't bite, she'll get bored. 'Now why would you think a thing like that?'

'Because you're saving all your rotten books for them, that's why!'

There was an almost sacred sort of silence, a deep

echoey one, as I tried to take in what the fiend was saying. 'What books?' I finally choke.

Man, she's been waiting for this little opening. She goes at me like dry rot. 'All those soppy ballet and pony stories. Nan lets me read them when you're out to lunch for about four hours – is that why you're so fat, because you eat lunch for four hours?'

'I'm *curvaceous* because I take the contraceptive pill. I take the contraceptive pill because men want to have sex with me. Don't worry, you ugly little sow, it's never going to happen to *you*.' I've totally lost it now. Just in case you hadn't noticed.

She sniggers. 'I've had sex with three men already. One of them was a member of BUPA.'

'That'll come in useful,' I snarl. 'When I perforate your eardrum.' I'm shocked, I really am. Sex at twelve: that's what it's like these days. When I was twelve, the nearest I ever came to sex was doing the splits at my ballet class.

Of which more from Michaela right now: 'Yeah, all those soppy ballet stories. And ponies.' She smirks again. 'That's about right, come to think of it. A load of old pony, that's what they are.'

I am silent. Trying to comprehend betrayal as massive as my grandmother's is no easy task.

'D'you know what pony means?' Michaela asks helpfully. 'It means –'

'I know what "pony and trap" means, thank you very much,' I say wearily. 'I haven't spent half my life in this hellhole we call our capital without getting wise to the singularly graceless lingo of the natives.'

'Don't you like London, then?' This is the nearest the creature's ever come to sounding half-human, by the way. Obviously because it's had its triumph now and can relax at last.

For the first time, I wonder. 'Your name's "Kemp", isn't it, Michaela?'

'Yeah,' she says suspiciously.

'And do you by any chance know the origin of your august family name, Michaela?'

'No.' She looks panicky. She knows I've got her now.

'It means thug. Boxer. Bare-knuckled fighter.' I lean so close to the little beast I can smell the Cream Soda Hubba-Bubba on its breath. 'But definitely not the sort of person who'd be let into BUPA. Savvy?'

She shrinks from me. I must have ring-flash eyes by now, I feel so incandescent with anger.

'Where is the darling old lady in both our lives, anyway?' I ask, too casually, starting to draw again. I'm giving my cyber-Erté an automatic rifle in the hand not holding the joint. 'Down the launderette showing off her shrivelled ovaries?'

'You're disgusting,' Michaela hisses. 'She's gone down the chippy!'

'How very appropriate, in your case –'

'She says I'm to set the table –'

'Go on and set it then. There are some extra-sharp knives in that top drawer there . . .'

Off she mooches, shooting little arrows of hate over her shoulder at me, and I sit there at my board, staring off into thin air, tapping a pencil against my teeth. Before long Liza comes in, shaking a wet umbrella all over my good wood floor.

'I'm 'ome, my love!' she yells, and guess what? She certainly isn't talking to me! 'I got us a nice bitta plaice, with a nice dollop of –' Then she finally clocks me. 'Oh. 'Ullo. Thought you'd be going out to dinner.'

'I may well be going out to *dinner*, Gran,' I smile quite pleasantly under the circumstances, 'but not to *lunch*. Which would appear to be what you have tucked in there under your armpit. Lunch. For two.'

'I thought thee'd be out, I tell 'ee,' she says, taking off her mouldy old coat. She won't let go of this coat; you'd think Kurt Cobain shot himself wearing it. Or Al Bowlly, or whoever was the crooning idol of her long-gone day. 'Thass why I only got two fish lots.' She takes her fetid purchases to the black-ash table – I know it's really Eighties, but hey, we're still living in the Eighties in our house: fast drugs, bad champagne and for all I know incipient herpes if that slag Siobhan's half the girl they say she is – and starts to unwrap them. 'Mick!' she calls.

'Just a mo, Nan!' it calls lustily from the toilet. Let's hope it slips on the marble tiles while it's purloining my Eau d'Hadrian and breaks its little neck, shall we?

'Gran, can I talk to you for a minute, please?' I say with rising hysteria. I look around wildly, and Michaela comes whistling out of the john, stinking of Byzance. 'In the toilet?'

This is the thing about living in a loft space. It looks lovely in glossy pictures in magazines when it's just you and the squeeze. It's nice when you've got a bunch of girls over and you're all half-cut and completely shameless and you all know each other's secrets anyway. But woe betide you if you want to whisper in someone's ear, and, let's face it, who amongst us doesn't from time to time? It's the lavatory or nothing.

'In the lavvy?' Liza rolls her eyes at Michaela. Who

giggles. Funny, with those cankerous cataracts, you'd think she'd be a bit limited in this department. But she's as fluent in eye-rolling as any Steppin Fetchitt parody. It's nice to have a talent, isn't it? 'If I must . . .'

'Oh dear, what can the matter be?' Michaela starts to sing, 'Two old ladies locked in a lavatreee –'

'Bless 'er,' says Liza as I lock the bathroom door. Her voice and face change from pure Andrex to harshest Izal as she turns to me. She puts down the toilet seat and perches on it impatiently. 'Spit it out, then.'

'They stayed there from Monday till Saturday –'

'Gran.' I try to speak calmly. 'Have you by any chance been giving your . . . friend my books to read?'

'Nobody knew they were there!'

'What books?' she says innocently, but her eyes creep towards the exit. Which I'm blocking.

'The ones I k-keep in that b-box under my bed.' Horrifically, I'm starting to blub. 'My b-ballet books. *Return to Sadler's Wells. Drina Dances in Exile. Jill's Gymkhana. The Twins at St Clare's. And* all my Malory T-Towers books.'

''Appen I might 'ave done.' She stands up and looks at me with real scorn. 'Yeah. So what?' Then, unforgivably, she sniggers. 'Thee biss getting a bit old for 'em now anyway, bissn't thee?'

I can't believe this. That the woman I believed loved me more than anyone on earth is really such a callous, uncaring, practically psychopathic old bitch. 'Gran!' I'm frightened I may strike her, and I have to take a step backwards. 'Those books are not just *books*, you know!' I take another step backwards, and fall over sprawling into the shower stall. As I fall my hand hits the tap and turns the cold spray on full.

'Mick!' Liza yells, literally screaming with laughter. 'Quick! Come and look at this! You never seen nothing so funny in all yer life!'

I lie there, and I cry.

Chapter **Eight**

'Are they,' said Dr Alibhai with some interest, 'first editions, these books? I imagine they must be very –'

'No!' I felt pretty embarrassed, to be honest. 'They're not valuable – not in the conventional sense. They're just, like, regular paperbacks, about ballet and horses and things. All little English girls read them. Well, used to. Before they started reading about serial killers and sodomites who chase cheerleaders. Like that little angel Michaela does. I mean, didn't you – I don't know about your lot –' I stopped. It was starting to sound a bit rude.

Usha looked at me solemnly, and she folded her hands in her lap, and she said in a sort of *social worker* voice: 'No, we little Asian girls used to read books about temple dancing virgins and girls who ride elephants and stuff.' She laughed, then paused. 'Ice-skating was my big thing, actually. D'you remember *White Boots*?'

'Noel Streatfield!' I yelped. 'She wrote *Ballet Shoes*, too! God! I *love* that book!' I felt my face fall. 'All those orphans. And girls at boarding school. And living with vicious relatives and girls that picked on them – *tell* me about it. All of them being brave. Being heroines. Noel Streatfield and all those other women writers were trying to *warn* us, Dr Alibhai. About how brave we were going to have to be when we grew up.'

'You think so?'

'Yeah – it was like this really covert feminism. They were warning girls, in code as it were, that life was really going to suck as soon as they were women. The boredom. The hassle. The marital combat. I don't know why feminists insist on females being called "women" rather than "girls", do you, Usha? Girls are free. Women are wombs . . . wombs.'

'Steady on!'

I thought about it for a while, then spoke. 'I'll tell you something, doctor. That I've never told anyone else before. Except my friends. And once when I was stuck on a train in France with this American woman. D'you know what my idea of the most brilliant evening possible is?'

'Tell me.'

I took a deep breath. 'It's being all by myself, and knowing no one's going to knock on the door and make trouble. Because that's what life is, doctor, when people start knocking on your door; one long game of Knock-Out Ginger, with you as the victim. Well, it's being all by myself, and knowing no one's going to come over or even call – everyone but me's dead, let's say – and it's having a big bath – *not* a shower, which is what people have when they don't want to even *think* about their lives – and going to bed, BY MYSELF, at half-past seven. Winter's best, when it's really dark. And then I'd drink Tizer and eat Butterscotch Instant Whip and watch tape after tape of *The*

Singing Ringing Tree – or maybe *White Horses*, which was about the Spanish Riding School in Vienna, remember? (Why *did* they have a Spanish Riding School in Vienna? What *is* Spanish riding, when it's at home? Goring a bull to death from on horseback?) While I'm sort of half re-reading *Ballet Shoes*. That's my perfect evening, doctor. And d'you know why?'

'Why?'

'Because being perfect means *being a child*.'

'Why so, Nicola?'

'Well, children can't get married for a start, can they? That's *got* to be half-way to paradise.' I squirmed on her couch. 'It's funny – in fact it's so funny that it's not funny ha-ha but funny boo-hoo – but when I was a child, all I could think about was growing up and leaving home and staying out and having sex and taking drugs. And now, when I *can* do all of those things, I don't want to. I've done them to death. I just want to go back *there* again. Second childhood. Like Michael bloody Jackson.' I laughed. '*Pathétique, non?*'

'No.' She shook her head. 'And quite common these days, I hear. Aren't there clubs where young adults go to play silly games like Twister?'

'Yeah, Siobhan's front room. No, it's called the Double Six Club. And get this, there's this *other* club where these people in like their twenties and thirties go and they *put on nappies and get into these giant cots and playpens and suck dummies*! Apparently they say it "relaxes" them! Well, I'm not going to play a featured role here as the pot who calls the kettle black, but I certainly don't go to those extremes, Usha, do I?'

I must have sounded like some daft little girl because

she laughed and said: 'No, Nicola, you certainly do not.'

'Then what's it all about, doctor? Is it the millennium, do you think?'

She sighed. I could have made stockings out of those sighs, and sold a million. 'I really don't know, Nicola.' Then she was rifling in the drawer for something; it turned out to be a battered, half-empty box of Jaffa Cakes (Classic). She stood up and reached across her desk, and I sort of hung off my couch, and we exchanged prisoners. She takes a quarter of my income a month, I take a stale old Jaffa Cake with most of the Jaffa somewhat sinisterly sucked or syringed out – but hey, it's the thought that counts. '*Noggin the Nog* does it for me. *Noggin the Nog*, and Jaffa Cakes.'

I lay back, sucking my Jaffa Cake like a baby with a rusk. Which, without its Jaffa *raison d'être* and most of its choccy exfoliated by Time, the great vandal and demonic beautician, it quite resembled.

'And I *dream*, doctor . . .'

What do I dream of? The usual psychic overspill, tossed in the celestial skip of the unconscious. One night I dreamt a dream which seems so egotistical that, if you stuck it in a novel to illustrate how egotistical the dreamer was, crowds would gather below your window and yell up: 'Oh, *please*! Easy on the old metaphor there!'

Here's my egotistical dream: I dreamt that Hugh Grant and Elizabeth Hurley were both in love with me. Not just that, but they were actually *knocking on my door for it*. And I was cringing beside the big bed, the big bed which can be colder than Canada and hotter than hell, trying to crawl under it, and begging of Matt – yes! I could tell it was indeed a dream, and not reality, because Matt was at home! – to please, *please*, make them go away! *Please* make them leave me alone!

I'll give you three guesses what Matt did. Did he: a) stride to the door and beat off the ravening beasts with his bare hands; b) the above, but making sure he got a few decent shots of their reluctant retreat; or c) lick his lips and say, 'Hey, come on, babes. We're all adults here, aren't we?' Which in my experience is what grown men say when they're just about to behave like twelve-year-old masturbators granted three wishes.

With just a Chubb lock safeguarding my chastity, Hughie and Liz were going bananas. I could hear their pukka voices going fuck-crazy. 'But *I* saw her first, Lizzie!' 'Sod you, H! She smiled at me in the Groucho ladies' absolutely *aeons* before she ever set eyes on you!'

I started to cry and attempted to crawl under the bed, not easy with my thighs and only four inches of leeway. I had my fingers in my ears, and I just knew that Hughie and Liz would envy my ears like mad if only they knew. 'Please, Matt!' I begged, 'please make them go away!'

But he was simultaneously loading his camera and taking off his trousers. 'Just a quick one,' he said, as he tap-danced across the room to open the door.

I *told* you it was egotistical. But it was just a one-night stand. Most of my sex dreams are about – get this – my husband.

It's the same dream every time. We're making love

and his long hair is getting in my face. He stops, looks at me and says: 'Is my hair getting in your face?'

'Yes.'

And he puts it back in a bandeau.

When I told Zoë this dream, she just looked at me amazed. 'And?'

'And then we went on doing it.'

Zoë shook her head. 'You know what's sad? That you're not even making it up. That you're not even a fantasist. Because this stuff is just *too mind-blowingly boring to make up*. You're fucking your own husband, and his hair gets in your eyes –'

'Face.'

'– *so he ties it back*! Do you have any germ of comprehension, however slight, of what an impoverished waking life you lead if this is what happens when your mind is let off its tether?'

So I dream about Hugh Grant and Elizabeth Hurley (sex with, avoiding) and I dream about Matthew (sex with, getting; unmanageable hair, controlling). These dreams are pretty damn easy to get a handle on: I dream of being desired, I dream of being considered. But there are other dreams, the ones not about sex. And they're the ones I find so shocking, so private, so something wild.

I'm a child – yes, you saw that one coming, didn't you? I'm a child and I'm running through a field of golden corn. It's cartoon corn, corn silk, soft as satin as I cut a shimmering swathe through it. Somewhere there's music, and the song is – try, *try* to remember – the song is 'Try to Remember'. ('Try to remember, the kind of September . . .') As sung by Nat 'King' Cole. (I never liked those quotes. Like somebody gave him the nickname who thought he was crap. It's hard to imagine that there was a time when quotation marks weren't about irony, but about respect.)

I'm laughing as I run, and butterflies swoop around me, landing on my hair and shoulders, living jewellery. The sun is Sixties, going on Seventies. And then I come to a sudden stop, and stand there panting for breath, gazing at something in complete rapture. We can't see right now what it is.

And then the camera swoons and stumbles and then pirouettes, staring over the shoulder of the child Nicola as she gazes transfixed at the thing she has been running towards, without even knowing it: a picture-book riverbank, too beautiful to be true. With kingfishers.

And how does this dream of dreams always end? Not with benediction. Not with baptism. Not with being born again. It ends, without fail, this way:

'Nic'la! I've bin an' gone and wet meself!'

'So you're running.' Her delicate shell-likes really perked up at this one. *Here* we go, Freud or foe. 'Who's chasing you?'

'No one!' I said crossly. 'Honestly, Usha, does everything have to be rape, rape, rape around the clock with you people? I'm not running *from* anything.' I thought about it, which was obviously more than *she* had. 'Or *to* anything, unless you count the river which seems pretty bloody obvious. It's just about ... beauty. And innocence. And, like, the two of them together are what being a child is all about, aren't they?'

'So you did a good deal of this sort of thing when

you were a child, did you, Nicola? Running through meadows –'

'Cornfields –'

'Through cornfields down to rivers . . .'

Of course, I was about to answer, 'Yes!' – because this dream was so real and regular – but then the actual facts hit me round the face like a wet kipper and I said sulkily: 'No. To be honest, Usha, I can't say for sure that I actually *ever*, like, remember running through a cornfield or indeed any sort of field to a river. Though to be fair there were lots of both on the outskirts of Bristol. No . . . I suppose I was more into staying in my bedroom . . . drawing, painting. Making inept wax dollies of June Bolan and Angie Bowie and sticking safety pins into them. (We didn't have pins proper, I told you this. Vis-à-vis the Catherine Wheel class-crisis.) Looking in the mirror, never quite coming to a logical conclusion about whether I was the most brilliant person in the world or the worst. Being plain and awkward, and drawing myself anyway, and then somehow becoming sort of beautiful. I was like a work of art, Usha, that somehow *painted itself* – all through the long hot back-bedroom summer holidays, with the curtains drawn. They were purple.' I stopped for five seconds, then went on. 'When girls from school used to come and call for me at weekends or during those holidays – presumably in order to force me to run through a field to a river, doctor; I never quite asked – I used to shut myself in my bedroom and beg my mum to tell them I was ill so they'd go away. Usually I had a bilious attack. Pretended I did, I mean.' I laughed, and I really did find it funny, and certainly not 'bittersweet' or any of those noncy get-outs. 'I must have had more bilious attacks than anyone in the whole of Avon County!' I felt my face fall. 'Only it was Somerset then.'

'Didn't your mother mind lying?'

No more than yours did lying to the Immigration Department, dollface! No, that's a dreadful thing to think. She can't help being a subcontinental snootbag. 'Well – it didn't exactly bust her buttons, but she knew that if she forced me to go out with these Top Shop zombies then I really *would* have a bilious attack. And a half! I suppose she thought she may as well be hung for a sheep as a lamb. Or is it a goat?' I shrugged. I couldn't think about animal rights right now. 'Whatever.'

'Right.' I can *hear* her suppressing a smile. 'And so. How are events progressing with your grandmother?'

Pushy, pushy, pushy. Cheers, Usha! I sighed, and made the ultimate sacrifice – I told the truth. 'Not too good. And now Matt's coming back . . .'

I didn't actually witness it with my own eyes, but I *knew* how Matt would look on the cab ride from the airport to home. It didn't matter how many times Siobhan's brilliant thighs got a hold on him in a way that the Undertaker, Papa Shango and Hit-Man Hart couldn't come close to even working together; we had chemistry. He walked into a room, and I was literally undone: I came unravelled, like crap, inaccurate knitting. The Nicole and Nicola I was with other people, no matter how well it seemed to hold together or progress, was shown up in all its cack-handed water-treading mediocrity when Matt and I looked at each other. Every time we saw each other, we were shocked; that's the best way I can say it.

I can picture him in the taxi, and it is almost as poignant for me as picturing him in Siobhan's mouth, because if we're going to be completely honest I feel a glint of jealousy towards everything he touches. Sure, the leather of the seat isn't alive now – but it *was*. And he's sitting on it! I mean, Siobhan isn't alive *as such* – she's not *sentient*. Which means that she and the seat are much of a muchness. When you're in love, really in love, all the world is the other woman.

But, faithless or not, I know he wants me. Matt must be – I'm being creative here – the only man on earth who thinks about his wife while he's shagging his girlfriend. What does he call her when he comes, you might wonder – Siobhan, or Bridget? Neither. He calls her *Nicole*.

He's coming home, and he's bought me orchids, and he looks younger than ever, and he loves me. He misses his *wife* – and to miss your wife, if you love her, is romantic and epic and scary in a way that missing your girlfriend never can be. Think about it: from one angle, making a woman your wife domesticates and corrals her. From another, it makes her far more lethal, far more likely to lead to mayhem and Hemingway.

'You slept with my girlfriend.' (Result: girlfriend is utter slag. Let's go down pub and pull. Easy come, easy go.)

'You slept with my wife.' (Result: Quentin Tarantino film. From hell.)

'My girlfriend's left me.' (Result: girlfriend is utter bitch. Let's go down pub etc.)

'My wife's left me.' (Result: probable suicide. Or join Men's Group, long-game version of same.)

'I've got a girlfriend. I really want to be faithful to her.' (Result: could go either way, depending on amount of vodka consumed.)

'I'm a married man.' (Result: complete and utter fuckfest.)

But I know, I *know* he loves me. After all this time, he's even slightly physically excited – yes! – as he pays off the cab driver, and that's not a sexy scenario. He's thinking of me, and his mouth is drier than he can rationalise, as he climbs the stairs, because Liza's left the lift grille open again.

Home. *Home*. To Matthew, right now, no word has ever sounded more sensual. He unlocks the door; even the feeling of the key in the lock makes him shiver. He enters the room; even entering a room makes him bite his lip, thinking of how Nicole will bite his lips, and hers, as he enters her.

Liza sits watching the wrestling. Guinness bottles fall at her feet as grandchildren once did.

And Nicole, for the first time in her life so far as he knows, is at the ironing board. And she is ironing a pig's head.

A pig's head.

She looks at him with horror and resignation mixed, not a look she's big on. He looks back at her, aghast. He lays the orchids on the floor very slowly, as on a grave, then quietly closes the door as he leaves.

It's later, much later . . .

'Kiss me! *Kiss me!*' The only time our open mouths make any sense these days is when we kiss. The spoken word – man's triumph over the beasts – forget it. Kissing is the *real* difference. The spoken word is essentially as vulgar, self-seeking and brutish as the canine habit of sticking your nose up someone's BTM.

Matt and I kiss, with such irritation and passion that we hurt each other immediately.

'Fuck! Watch it, will you? You've knocked a corner off my tooth!'

'Shut the fuck up, Nicole!'

This is the way we used to kiss when we were courting, when I was with Remi. Our kisses were like violent, resentful domestic quarrels between married people: No, it's *your* turn to take out the garbage! We kissed as though divorce lawyers were urging us on, eager to see us maul each other. We kissed often without any real pleasure, just desperate to draw sustenance from each other. Our kisses were not lush, photogenic affairs; we were not Liz and Monty in *A Place in the Sun*. If I moved too much, or relaxed into it, Matt with a hiss of impatience would grab my face, force my head back against the wall and apply his mouth to mine as thoroughly as a paramedic giving the kiss of life to his grandchild. Often, if we hadn't been together for a while, Matt would manufacture a huge amount of saliva before kissing me and feed it to me matter-of-factly throughout. I lapped it up, in every sense. After kissing, we could barely look at each other; we were gorged, full up, shut down.

We're kissing that way now, Matt's spittle as steady and essential to me as an intravenous drip. The completeness of my desire for him gives me a weird sort of detachment: I'm so totally ready, holding nothing back nor working towards something, that I see myself from outside. We seem to be fighting each other, our ability to melt into the other bringing out some reflexive self-preserving mechanism. I push at his shoulders as he mounts me; he turns his head away.

'Fuck you, Nicole!'

'No, fuck you!' I gasp with wonder as he's inside me once again. You know how you know you're in love? Every time feels like the last.

'Fuck me, Nicole, fuck me!' Every stroke is a revelation; every thrust a confirmation. That's a lot of everys.

'Oh, Matt – fuck, fuck, *fuck*!'

'Oi!' comes the cry. 'Language!'

Chapter **Nine**

I am *in love*. *In* love. I like the 'in', and I think it really means something. When something's good for us, we're *at* it: at work, at home, at school, at peace, at ease. When something's bad for us, we're *in* it: in trouble, in debt, in jail, in love. In Queer Street. Being in love, badly, so it hurts, is like being in some sort of queue that never ends. You're just waiting, for ever, for it to be over, so you can start to live again. Except – you always forget this bit – that, when it is over, your life goes all limp, becomes all boring and difficult to wear, like a piece of clothing where the elastic's snapped. Out of love, you are a floppy Dali watch. You are killing time, waiting for the assassin who will bring you back to life. You are a working pilot, apparently sane and respectable, who dreams only of being hijacked.

You are a plane that wants to make a crash-landing.

You are a crash dummy who dreams of losing his limbs.

You are a dummy.

You are Nicole.

*

We sit in another taxi, and we are miles apart. No Knowledge can bring us back together right now.

I look out of the window. There's nothing there, just a countdown. 'And I really don't know why we had to come out this evening, either. I've got work to do – *I've got a career, too, you know*! Those new pastels I ordered came, and the Japanese paper. Why couldn't we just have a sandwich at home?'

'What sort of sandwich?' He's loving this. 'Pig?'

'You eat bacon, don't you?' I'm not going to be hit over the head with this one. 'You pig it, in fact! Where d'you think *that* comes from? D'you think it grows on trees?'

'It's not the same, Nicole!' He flicks at his hair like a stupid tart. (Probably called Siobhan. Though christened Bridget.) 'My God! The way it *looked*!'

'Oh yes, the way it looked! That's all that really matters, isn't it? The way anything *looks*!' I'm well away. 'Especially *women*.'

'I wasn't talking about women, was I? I was talking about . . . pigs' heads! And the women who . . . *iron them*!' He shakes his own head, the pig. 'Nicole, Nicole . . . you really didn't see it from where I was standing. It looked like . . . I don't know. Like something by some Surrealist on a monumentally bad acid trip. Like some filthy German video at the ICA that we'd walk out of after five minutes.'

He *knows* he only has to mention the Germans to make me see a red mist. (I don't know why. I think Emma and Zoë may be sort of one-third Jewish, but it's not that, is it? It's being *English*. Cats and dogs hate each other; so do English and Germans. Thank God, thinking about it! If it ain't broke, why fix it? –

Hey, I bet you never heard a *dentist* say that.) 'She's been off her food for five days, Matt! When I said I'd get her anything she wanted, I wasn't to know she'd ask for a pig's head, was I? And I certainly didn't imagine I'd have to *iron* it first.'

'You never iron anything for me,' says Sulky-Boots, getting to the root of the problem. And then, of course, obscuring it. 'Nicole. Just think for a second. Can you even *imagine* what ironing a pig's head does to your karma?'

'I don't know about my karma. But it's ruined my bloody iron.' I look at Matt's profile. He is smiling, trying not to. Compared to him I'm a comic fucking genius, it's true. 'So who else is going to be at this dinner?'

'Just a few cool people. Cobblers . . .'

'God, they're your friends, aren't they? I'd hate to hear how you talk about your enemies!'

He has to laugh. (Or he'd cry?) 'I meant they're shoemakers. Su and Lu.'

'I'm just guessing now, Matt.' (I am, too), 'but would I be right in guessing that Su and Lu do not spell their names with the normal number of vowels?'

He laughs again. 'What a clever girl you are, Nicole. S.U. And L.U.'

'Why do people do that, do you think?'

'I don't know.'

'I mean, would you call yourself Matt with an M.H.A.T.?'

'No.' He's still laughing.

'Or listen. I've got an idea. To fit in with your cool friends, I could be Nicole with an N.I.K.K.A.L.L.E. Which sounds like a sportswear company.'

His eyes are closed, he's laughing silently, dead relaxed at last.

'And Siobhan could be S.H.I.V.A.W.N. Or perhaps, even more literally, C.U.N.T.'

His eyes are open, but closed off, looking at me as though I've said something racist about Stevie Wonder. Like, 'He's blind!'

'Leave it, Nicole.'

'And Jonh with the H will be there? Jonh with the H after the N, not before?'

'Yeah.' Defensively, the homo cretin. 'He's a great guy.'

'Fine. I can dig dyslexics.' I look out of my window. 'And who will be the lovely Jonh's dinner date?'

I can just *hear* him weighing up whether or not to tell me. Finally he speaks: 'Siobhan, I think.'

There's this icy silence. I breathe hot huff on my window, and I write I HATE on the misty backdrop. Then I say: 'Excuse me. But is this Siobhan any relation whatsoever to Siobhan O'Thing, the teenaged mannequin of your acquaintance? That is, the one with the brain of Bertrand Russell and the cleavage of Jane? Or is it the one with the mind of Claud Cockburn and the face of Claudia Schiffer? I forget, you see – there seem to be so many models these days who are as brilliant as they are beautiful. Oh – no! – hang on, will you? It's not the same Siobhan O'Thing who you were snapping in expense-account Paradise a couple of weeks ago, is it?' I snap my fingers, badly. I'm in love, I tell you. I've lost all my gifts, even that one. '*What* a coincidence! I never would have thunk it!'

'Leave it, Nicole.' He holds his forehead in his hand.

The Thinker. I *don't* think. 'OK? She's a great girl, I'm telling you. You'll love her . . .'

'Will I?' Even now wanting to be convinced. Wanting to believe. Lookabye! Gullible bitch at twelve o'clock!

'Everyone does . . .'

Now that, that was the wrong thing to say. To a woman in therapy. A woman in her thirties. A woman who's got her grandmother sleeping in her bed. Yes, that really, really was the wrong thing to say, thank you, Matt! Of course I go into Major Cow mode. 'Oh, I'm *sure* they do. Tell me, Matt. Do her boyfriends take a number and line up, like in that New York deli we were in last time?'

He's silent for a while. Then he snaps: 'At least she hasn't got her grandmother sleeping in her bed!'

I look at him, insouciant I hope, then turn slowly to stare out of my window. At nothing, for no one: 'How do you know?'

'I . . . I just presumed. Naturally.'

I just keep on looking, not seeing.

He puts his hand on my knee: 'Nicky . . .'

'Please don't.' I say it sweetly as I remove his hand. 'I'd really rather you wouldn't. Not after your hands have been all over the cold meats counter.'

Su and Lu are a cross between Hänsel and Gretel (without the worldly wisdom) and Laurel and Hardy (without the blatant sex appeal). They sit there giggling and holding hands like they've just snogged behind the bike sheds for the very first time a couple of hours earlier, despite the fact that neither of them will ever see forty again and they've been married (to each other) for even longer than Dreamboat and I. Cobblers in Love; not an attractive idea, is it?

Su's what they call a 'Big Woman'. So big, in fact, that it's a wonder I don't like her. It's not every day another woman makes you feel like the most sylph-like, desirable creature on Earth without even putting her paw on your thigh. But, goodness gracious *moi*, that's certainly the effect old Su has on me! I could kiss her, if she wasn't so incandescently stupid and physically repulsive. This Lu, he's like the size of one of her forearms. The thought of them having sex makes me think of that line from 'The Hokey-Cokey' – you know, the one that goes 'You put your whole self in, your whole self out'!

Excuse me, did I say Su 'makes' me feel thin and desirable? Ah. Wrong tense, I see. I should have said that Su 'made' me feel thin and desirable. Just by sitting there, looking like some sort of European food mountain. Until the moment, that magical moment, when Siobhan O'Thing entered the room, Jonh with the tardy H following five steps behind like a Muslim bride.

Now I've seen models in the flesh before. I was once in love with a boy called Mark Kaplan when I was in my last year at St Martin's. Mark Kaplan was one of those weird Jewish boys who looks like the WASPiest aristocrat in the world; there's just one in every generation, and I guess the female equivalent would be Lauren Bacall. For some reason this Mark person never cottoned on that I was A over T in love with him, even though I once crawled under his desk when I was drunk one afternoon with the intention of sucking him off while he designed a post-modern cathedral. He just looked under the table at me, smiled his brilliant smile and said: 'Hi, Nicky. Have you lost something?'

Yes! I wanted to scream. Yes, I've lost my fucking heart! And I've got reason to suspect that it might have migrated into your 501s. Take them down so I can have a quick shufti, will you?

'Pencil,' I muttered, crawling tragically backwards.

Anyway, I lived with the low-level misery of unrequited love for several months, sustained by the fact that this Kaplan type wasn't letting anyone else, man, woman or beast, suck him off either. Then one Monday he came into class smirking like a maniac; by lunchtime it was all over the school. *Mark Kaplan had got off with a Page 3 girl!*

This would have been front-page stuff in any working or learning environment you can imagine – except Stringfellows, where *not* getting off with a Page 3 girl over the weekend would have been a major talking point. There would naturally be a lot of 'Whooah!' across the reeking urinals, and other general squalidness. But at St Martin's, there was the whole camp angle too, of course. For some reason I found this far more upsetting than the predictable ribaldry; was sleeping with a Page 3 girl camp, or was it kitsch? Girls debated the subject elegantly as they backcombed their hair and slicked on lipstick in the ladies'. It's neither! I screamed silently from inside my cubicle in hell. It's neither! *It's an act of unbridled evil which should be punishable by death!*

So I did my best for a solid three weeks, mooching around Mark Kaplan and dishing out looks which should have killed by the dozen. Not that he noticed. He had smirked himself into a state of stupefaction which closely resembled the plateau stage of cultist brainwashing. It's a wonder he didn't hole up in St Martin's with a vast array of weaponry and his fucking Page 3 girl and demand an infinite supply of white stilettos and a plane to take them to Tenerife.

Then, at an end-of-term party which I had been thinking of for weeks as an end-of-tether party, I saw her. I'd say he wore her on his arm, only she'd have had to be on stilts to reach it. No, he wore her on his *thigh*, sort of, which she could just about reach. Short? Put it this way: if she knelt down to give him a blow job, it would have ended up as a toe job. Bad hair? For some reason, it made me think of the way a woman's hair might look two days after she'd had an abortion. Short legs? She made Douglas Bader look like Cyd Charisse.

But old Mark Kaplan didn't give a damn. He paraded that troglodyte around as though she really was the belle of the ball, introducing her to all and sundry like an affianced Southern gent. I stood there, nineteen, more beautiful than I'd ever be, blonde, five-ten in heels, and clutched at the arm of my best friend Holly so violently that she was bruised beyond belief next day. Holly was the poshest girl I'd ever known, and the prettiest, and the sweetest. Her father was the ninth or nineteenth richest landowner in England or Europe, I forget which; and as I stood there mutilating her, she closed her hands over my fingers to comfort me, thus encouraging me to dig even deeper in.

'It's a joke, it's a joke,' she said through clenched teeth as I marked her perfect skin for ever, 'just a fucking joke, like in those John Belushi films. It's a pig party!' Holly looked a lot like Darcey Bussell; the sight of us, so beautiful, so baffled, was truly a sight to remember, some guy told me later, drunk of course:

'That was the big obsession in our set: to fuck Holly or Nicky, preferably both. In our *dreams* of course you did it together first, then held out your arms to us. But as time went on, the more you both despised us and the more you just needed each other. That night Mark brought Alison to the party – I'm sorry, Nic, because I don't feel that way now – anything that was left of our dreams came true. We saw the look on your face, and the way Holly was at last completely useless to you. And later that night, towards the end, in the john, someone said to me: "Well – I guess Holly and Nicky got fucked, finally. And fucked by a plug-ugly Page 3 girl, at that." '

But get a load of this – Siobhan doesn't look like Alison. Here's a weird fact: there are ugly models and plain models and beautiful models, just the way there are ugly women and plain women and beautiful women. It's all to do with the camera.

Siobhan (Bridget) is just irrevocably beautiful. I really, really believe that she's not wearing make-up; when most models are allegedly *au naturel*, it's taken a Korean working week. But I can see her freckles, and the curtain call of a blemish on her chin; she's so perfect that she can flaunt her imperfections. In fact, she wears them like expensive moleskin beauty spots, the type they wore in the eighteenth century.

She's all of a piece, serenely seamless, the way truly beautiful women always are. *She hasn't been put together – she came that way!* She didn't have to learn to be no woman, the way those old-time chain-smoking philosopher-brown-nosing French feminists used to say. She was *born* like it! As easy and unfair as being born a dolphin. And here she is, throwing it all at me as though I'm the first human being she's ever met after a lifetime of being raised by antisocial wolves in Belgium. Like I'm *someone*.

'Nicole? Matt's Nicole? Oh, excellent! I've heard *so much* about you!'

I smile bravely, wriggle in my chair and beckon her close. She turns her perfect, visibly smirking ear to my bad mouth. I giggle like a cretin, or a girrrl: 'Oh, he's such a blabbermouth! There isn't anyone who's anyone in this town who doesn't know he gave me chronic recurring herpes before it was even fashionable!'

She pulls back, rippling like a sumptuous beige Slinkee. She sits down opposite me – all the better for kicking her in the positively Stakhanovite crotch, I register objectively – and Matthew Miller, who's apparently the man I married many years ago, gives us the old one-two. It's like he's the jockey, I'm the old nag and she's the jump: You're not going to do anything silly and *refuse*, are you, darling? Come on, play the game! When I dig my heels in, remember we're a team and let's just *get over this*.

'Well, it's *brilliant* to meet you, actually.' She recovers well, old Bridge, I'll give her that. Let's hope she recovers that quickly from a dose of syphilis or a punch up the bracket. Both of which she is scheduled to get sort of soonish if she keeps on messing with my worst half. 'Because I mean, I *really* love women.

They're so much *nicer* than men. Especially African ones. Don't you agree, Nicole?'

'No, not really.' I indulge in a little light smouldering over the twelve types of lettuce salad. Twelve, for the sake of fuck! Is that a good working definition of 'Life's too short' or what? 'So many of them seem to have a nasty habit of shagging my husband.'

From the corner of my eye I see him splutter into the butter. Siobhan looks shocked. But even shocked she's fully finished, undiminished. Fuck.

Matt pulls himself together with the hysterical efficiency of an air hostess organising a kamikaze jump. For charity, of course. 'We've got Nic's grandmother staying with us,' he says. As though that explains everything. As though Liza was the gypsy with the golden tooth brewing Love Potion Number Nine down on 44th and Vine and then pressing it on to him and Siobhan in a fit of bloody-minded philanthropy. Whooah – good one, Matthew. Bloody dirty realism run riot.

'Oh!' Siobhan's had another idea; bloody *Birth of a Nation* Part Two. 'I *love* old people too! They've just been *around* such a long time! Isn't that why they're so *wise*, Nicole?'

'Oh yes. Clever as a cartload of monkeys.' Please. I didn't ask to be born. I *especially* didn't ask to be born so I could end up at a dinner party with a squad of characters who think that searching out and serving up twelve types of lettuce isn't necessarily proof of imminent cretinism.

Matt takes my hand under the table. Hugs my hand, rather. You know the way one consenting adult sometimes takes another consenting adult's hand under the table? As the opening step, the starting pistol, of the famous old fisted glove? Of love? Well, this isn't it. This is the bloody straitjacket of conjugal common sense. Of 'Steady as she goes, old girl!' This is the sort of hand-holding that gets committed at that crucial marital phase where monogamy slowly but surely fades into celibacy.

Or rather, adultery. Because as I turn and my glance flickers past Matthew to Siobhan, I see her lotus-eating, locust-spitting, cock-sucking, photographer-rimming mouth make an O of photogenic pleasure, and I know, as sure as models never eat meat except in bed, that she too has been honoured with his hand. Surely *this* wasn't what that clever book I bought but never read, as per, was banging on about? *Becoming Digital?*

It kills me the way cigarettes have to come with a warning printed on them. That they'll do for you. Why don't men come with a warning on them, then? Because for sure they'll give you a lot more than the Big C. The Big VD, for one. Then there's the Big P (pregnancy, leading to tiny feet, patter of), the Big G (erosion of G-spot, thanks to endless clueless bashing away at it, as though they're doing ancient brass rubbings or something) and finally, once they've ruined you from top to toe, our old friend the Big E.

Drink could come with a warning or two as well, if you ask me. But it would have to be different warnings for different drinks, wouldn't it? And not going by boring old alcohol content, either, but by the very nature of the liquor being imbibed. Because different drinks *do* have different characters. As much as people. *More* than people, if you're lucky enough to hang with the deadbeats I've been honoured with in this, my one and only life.

I'll give you a for instance. Twelve-year-old Malt Whisky From the Island of Iona. Brewed by Druids or Whatever. Well, the warning would be: WARNING! DRINKING MALT WHISKY CAN SERIOUSLY DAMAGE YOUR TASTE IN KNITWEAR! YOU WILL BUY HALF A DOZEN CABLE-KNIT SWEATERS AND SPEND THE REMAINDER OF YOUR EVENINGS WEARING THEM IN FRONT OF AN OPEN FIRE ACROSS FROM A MAN CALLED GEOFF WHO BELONGS TO FAMILIES NEED FATHERS AND WHILE CLAIMING TO LOVE THE HUMAN RACE ACTUALLY HATES THE FEMALE HALF OF IT! ONE NIGHT, AFTER ONE WHISKY TOO MANY, HE WILL SODOMISE YOU AND COME ALL OVER YOUR CABLE-KNIT BACK!

Or there's vodka and Slimline: WARNING! DRINKING VODKA AND SLIMLINE CAN SERIOUSLY DAMAGE YOUR CONVERSATIONAL SKILLS! WHEN A SILK CUT CIGARETTE IS ADDED TO THIS LETHAL BREW, YOU WILL BECOME ONE OF THOSE WOMEN WHO SIT ABOUT WITH UP TO SEVEN OTHER SIMILAR SAD SOULS TALKING ABOUT WHAT BASTARDS MEN ARE! AND THEY NEVER GET BEYOND THAT! AT THE END OF EVERY MONTH THEY DECLARE THAT THERE'S MORE TO LIFE THAN MEN, AND THAT THEY'RE GOING TO LEARN JAPANESE OR KICK-BOXING! BUT THEY DON'T! INSTEAD THEY TAKE UP WITH A MARRIED MAN CALLED ROB, WHICH IS A JOB DESCRIPTION AS WELL AS A NAME, AND THEY SPEND THE NEXT YEAR TENDING THEIR BEDSORES AND SITTING BY THE PHONE! AND JUST AS THEY GET HANDED THEIR BUS PASS, THEY THINK: 'UH-OH. ROB

ISN'T GOING TO LEAVE HIS WIFE. BECAUSE SHE'S DEAD! IN FACT, BOTH OF THEM ARE!'

Then there's champagne. Champagne rhymes with cocaine, and for more reasons than so that campy old Noel Coward could fit them into a song together, I'll tell you. No, they're alike in lots of other ways. For instance, they're the first things you brandish when you're trying to steer someone *à la sac*. It's corny and tacky as all get out but it works, especially these days, because the *objet d'sac* takes it for granted that you know *they* know it's corny and tacky as all get out and they think you're treating them as your equal by having them in on the old ironic post-modern seduction routine. Well ha bloody ha – let them think that, but secretly, between you, me and the doorpost, we only bought the stuff in the first place because we thought they were a corny-and-tacky-as-all-get-out type who'd fall over backwards *à la sac* the second they got a whiff of it.

But another thing, the real thing, is that with cocaine and champagne you're not paying so much for what you get as for what you don't get. So firmly established in the canon of luxury are these confections, like cashmere or the Kelly bag, that there's never that *desperate* thing about seeking oblivion through them. But I mean, oblivion's oblivion; if we're applying a little light logic here – and, like cleavage or diamonds, *never* risk logic before luncheon, say I – then someone getting blind on Bolly is as desperate as someone getting blind on Chianti Mac.

But it doesn't *look* that way: cocaine and champagne always look like life's little luxuries, never white-knuckle necessities. So you're paying for freedom from addiction, to be the opposite of some poor character who gets a yen for Thunderbird and Temazepam when the sun goes down and it's playtime in the throbbing metropolis. Never mind the fact that your non-addiction is costing twenty times what his addiction is! So you end up working all the hours God sends just to break even with the fact that you're not addicted to anything! – Listen, I'm *sure* there's some parallel universe where it all makes sense.

So what you're paying for here is freedom from seeming desperate, and freedom from seeming addicted. Freedom from looking poor's going to come in here too, obviously. You're also paying for not having a hell-on-Earth hangover next day, either. But champagne, like cocaine, brings with its lush little self a whole nother set of problems whose real punch comes in not looking like problems in the first place.

Because champagne is a 'celebration' drink, we don't treat it with even the modicum of wariness we do all other tipples. It's something to do with the noise the cork makes, or the way the bubbles go up your nose like choicest Corona, but whatever it is it gets your guard down in a way no other hooch does. To turn down champagne seems churlish, seems too much like making a point, and one not worth making at that. So we swill it like lunatics whenever it comes our way.

I said earlier that salt and vinegar crisps tasted like regret; to me, after a certain point – somewhere halfway through the second bottle – champagne starts tasting like regret too. But it's that dirty, low-down, duplicitous regret which, for some reason too awful to even think about, makes you want nothing more than *to do that very thing again, right here and now*! Particularly sleep with the wrong person who you slept with once and have regretted it ever since. If you wanted to be coarse, I guess you could call it Wet Regret.

So are we destructive with our emotions, or what are we? When we get something beautiful, do we set out to destroy it? Or does it just happen, like perfume evaporating if you leave the top off? The jury's out on this one.

'Love is a lemming,' I said lushly one night to Lucy.

'Love is nothing of the sort,' she said briskly – this was before old Just William, mind you. 'Love is going to Sainsbury's every Saturday and being secure enough to buy non-brand-name goods in front of each other – even *beans*. It's walking in the rain holding hands. Boating on the Serpentine. And him pulling out and coming over your back when he buggers you because he knows *you don't like it up there*. So don't tell *me* about love,' she finished smugly.

But I digress! What sort of warning, pray, should good old bubbly bear? WARNING: DRINKING CHAMPAGNE CAN SERIOUSLY DAMAGE YOUR SENSE OF HUMOUR? SENSE OF IRONY? SENSE OF SELF? Because I can trace my present state of tosserdom, I'm pretty sure, right back to the time when I began to take champagne for granted.

Well, we've been at the old golden fizz tonight, Matt and I. And as we climb the stairs to our little nest, which by now isn't even spiritually or materially substantial enough to make into a nourishing Chinese broth, serves one, I can tell Lucy *one* new thing about love, at least: that it don't live here any more. It's been washed away, merrily, merrily, by a never-ending stream of Bolly and bile, white rum and come, Tizer and tears. It's beyond a joke, beyond repair, beyond redemption, this old love of mine. No need to leave the door on the latch or fashion a handy cat-flap for the velvet-pawed little blighter to slip silkily through in the heat of the night; it will never follow us up these stairs again. Love's left home, and it never, ever leaves a forwarding address. And not because it's *trying* to be difficult – but simply because it doesn't know where it's going to end up next. Except it's got a pretty good idea that it won't be Leeds.

I'm hissing at him as he fumbles with his right hand for the key he thinks is in one of his pockets. *Of course* I don't tell him he's holding it in his left hand. We're married, remember, and we hate each other. And, whatever else I am, I'm not a hypocrite.

'Your friend the dyslexic doesn't have much to say for himself, does he?' I hiss. 'Though of course, I suppose it was pretty hard for him to get a word in edgeways with Brain of Britain being there and all. Did you hear her when we were talking about that song, "On Top of Old Smokey"? The dumb twat actually, *actually* said, "Well, what was her true lover doing on top of Old Smokey anyway? Obviously she lost him because he was gay!" I bet the Brains Trust really felt like blowing *their* brains out when she decided to take up glamour modelling instead.'

'She's not a glamour model,' Matthew asserts wearily, finally fumbling his key into the lock. Even this drunken insertion of one and a half inches seems like a metaphor for his sex with Siobhan. And not even just a metaphor, come to think of it. *Miaow!* 'She was in *Elle* last month.'

'I'm sure she was.' I huff past him into our happy home, the House of Fun. 'And I'm sure you were the first to volunteer to go to *Elle* and back with her!'

'Nicole!' he hisses back, slamming the door. 'Will you just get *over* this thing with Siobhan?'

'Not till *your* thing gets over Siobhan, sweetheart!'

'You're a crazy paranoid, Nicole – I'm warning you! You should see a therapist, and soon!'

I haul off and hit the insensitive bastard. 'I *am* you pig! I *have been* for six months now!'

'Oh – yeah.' Any more sheepish and he'd have the Pure Wool symbol hanging off the end of his dick. Well, it is very soft these days. 'Right.'

'We don't have much to talk about though – me and Dr Alibhai,' I mock-muse. 'Seeing as she's the only woman in Greater London who you haven't shagged. The first few minutes of any session are always a bit awkward because we don't have the usual grab-bag of social chit-chat to toss around. Like whether you say "Whoops!" after you come in her mouth or "Take it, bitch! Take it all down!" Apparently it varies from shag to shag.'

'For God's sake stop using that word!' He's rifling in the drinks cupboard – I knew he would, and for this very reason all alcoholic beverages have been temporarily evacuated to the cupboard under the sink. Well, they always tell you to keep your marriage alive by ringing the changes. 'A shag is a type of tobacco. It has no place in the bedroom unless you're the kind of cliché-ridden cretin who smokes after sex.'

As I am, this really gets to me, of course. 'Oh! And I

suppose *that* bimbo calls it "making love"! Well, in my experience – which is admittedly nowhere near yours – the lower the act the more high-falutin' the language used to dress it up in. Me, I call a shag a shag.'

'I don't give a shag *what* you call it – there's precious little of it around here these days, is there? I thought modern marriage was about serial monogamy. I was prepared for that.' He stands up and slams the drinks cupboard shut. 'I didn't expect serial celibacy, though.'

Has he been reading my diary, or what? 'Oh, fuck off!' I aim the Quaker or Shaker chair at him and don't miss. He falls over, shrieking like a girl.

'Oi!' And here's Gran, just to make up the happy-clappy numbers, trailing in like Lady Macbeth in curlers. She plonks herself down in front of the TV and turns it on. 'Bloody racket!' She cracks open the can of Guinness she's clutching. ''Scuse French.'

'Hi, Gran!' I try to ignore the fact that Matt and I are currently in the middle of acting out some godforsaken Tennessee Williams play and attempt to turn it mid-scene into *The Little House on the Prairie*. 'Burning the candle at both ends? Or burning the midnight oil?'

'No I b'ain't.' She swigs on the Guinness and burps unpleasantly. 'Manners! No, I got the 'lectric on. You blind or summat?'

'Up late, I mean.' Out of force of habit, seeking shelter in sharpening pencils as usual – all the better to poke your husband's eyes out, I find – I walk towards my drawing board while Matt disappears into the toilet. No doubt to recreate the beauty and wonder of his many marriage-of-public-convenience liaisons with

Bridge-over-troubled-water. Come on, what d'you *expect* this time of night?

'Mick was 'ere.' As always upon speaking the Beloved's name, Gran perks up noticeably. 'Just went 'ome an 'alf an hour ago . . .'

'Just before the moon was full and she started growing hair on the palms of her hands, of course,' I jest. 'And how is the little dar –'

I stop suddenly. I stop suddenly because I have suddenly seen the absolute *mayhem* that is my work area. My beautiful new pastels, soft as Drew Barrymore's perineum, which I am currently missing one arm, one leg and one clitoris in order to meet the bill for, have been used to gang-rape Arnold Schwarzenegger, who obviously fought like the very Devil; my new Japanese paper, which I could only afford if I promised the physical equivalents from my first-born, has been used to clean up the dreadful damage wrecked upon Arnie's anal region, streaked as they are with all manner of deep reds, pinks and browns. I count, incredibly, to ten; under my breath: ten ways of slowly inflicting death upon the demon spawn that is Michaela Kemp, that is. And then, only then, do I go ballistic.

'Gran! GRAN!'

Look at her, turning in her chair and rolling her eyes as if I'm some sort of *bore* or something. 'Wass wrong *now*?' she sighs.

'What's WRONG?' I shout. 'What's *wrong*, you malign old witch? *Look*!' I gather together an armful of my extortionate debris, walk over to where Gran sits smirking and throw it, yes *throw it*, all over her. And doesn't it feel good! 'Look at these pastels!

Ruined! Look at this paper! *Japanese* paper! Trashed! Do you have any *idea* how much this stuff cost me? Do you have the *slightest notion* how *important* this job is to me?' I pause for breath, then go in for the kill. 'In fact, do you even have a *clue* about what it means to be a grown-up, adult human being? You *stupid* old woman!'

That does it. Liza's fists clench and she peers up at me from under the debris. 'Oooo! Old *woman*, is it now?'

Matt's coming out of the bathroom. But I'm unstoppable. 'Yes! *Old woman*!' I point at him for good measure. 'And here's another one! If *you* hadn't forced me to go out to dinner with your latest shag, you morally incontinent bastard, this would never have happened!'

Before I know it, while my attention is diverted to Matt, the senior member of the tag-wrestling team is on her buniony feet and grabbing me in a headlock, perfected by years of watching Ricky 'Twinkletoes' Starr and the Undertaker. 'Right, madam! – enough's enough!' She turns to Matt, wrenching my neck, it feels, from my collarbones. 'Matt! Get the carbolic from the kitchen, mate – we'll wash 'er mouth out!'

But while he's dithering, I break free. 'I'll wash *your* mouth out, you mean, you crumbling old crone!'

I lunge for her, and can feel her crêpey old skin under my fingers when Hubby Dearest comes between us, holding us apart: 'Whooah!'

I turn on him, clawing and cawing lividly. 'Let go of me, you! She's *my* grandmother!'

'That doesn't mean you get to beat her up all by

yourself,' he cracks weakly. (For a change.) 'Share and share alike!'

Maddened beyond belief, I scream: 'Oh! Yes, well, that's what they'll put on your tombstone, isn't it, *sweetheart*? If they can find a tent-shaped coffin to accommodate your permanent priapism, that is!'

'You crazy bitch!' he yells, instantly incensed. 'Can't you get this demented obsession with Siobhan off your mind for one second?'

'No! What's *your* excuse?'

I've never believed that lame line about there being a thin line between love and hate – obviously there's not, or we'd all go about on the verge of falling in love with the people we're married to. But one thing that the two states *do* seem to me to have in common is that when you're living them out, *acting* them out now, in our case, you become completely unaware of any other human presence whatsoever. It's just the three of you – the boy, the girl and the beef.

Whoever you terrify, whoever you maim or mentally maul to the death – that's not your problem when you're screaming blue mad at the wheel of your own injured ego. They're *roadkill*. Be they children being scarred for life with a ringside seat on the stairs, or a beloved grandmother condemned to live out her sunset years to the accompaniment of a hormone-driven cacophony of marital Mortal Kombat – *finish him*!

And so as my husband and I face up and face off for the final round, my grandmother does what innocent bystanders caught in the crossfire of domestic strife have done since the year dot: she turns on the television. And as she settles herself in for the night with her bottle of Guinness and her half-eaten bag of crisps (ready salted, like tears), I can *see* it, amazingly, out of the corner of my weary eye, coming up on the screen: THE BIG FIGHT – WELCOME BACK.

Chapter **Ten**

'I'm not imagining it, Usha – I just *know* I'm not.' I stubbed out my cigarette and she winced as though I was stubbing it out on one of her luscious old eyeballs. Think about it: you don't see many Asian babes smoking, do you? It's a real white-girl thing. Like thrush and fondues. 'D'you ever see that old black-and-white, *Gaslight*, where this guy's trying to drive Ingrid Bergman nuts? Well, he does it by insisting that she's *imagining* everything. The lights going out and stuff. Whereas *really* he's knocking off some little slag and he wants to get shot of her – Ingrid, I mean.'

'Yes. Right.' She hasn't heard a word I've said.

'Well, that's what *Matt's* trying to do with me. Pretend I'm imagining everything so everyone just thinks I'm a nutter.' I lit another one. 'But I *know* he's been shagging that spotty little slag.'

'Are you sure?' She smiled like a saint. Yeah, she knows too much to argue or to judge, old Dr Alibhai – just like that famous old feminist Bob Dylan said of his dream girl. But she doesn't know enough, unfortunately, to know that Matthew Miller is a screaming old slapper who would wedge his primary sex organ into a Jenga tower if the opening looked reasonably solid and seemed unlikely to tell his wife.

'Sure I'm sure.' I stopped to think, never a good idea. 'But even if I wasn't, it wouldn't really matter any more. The damage has been done. Done to *death*. We've rowed about it so much that the rows have become an end in themselves. If we stopped, what would we put in their place? Like all those couples who couldn't get along when the Vietnam War ended. Fighting's just about the one thing we've got left in common.'

'Some people say they are cathartic.' Dr Alibhai tosses me a line. Thanks, oh beauteous brown babe-type person, but the only line I want right now is white and is often-times sniffed up a fifty-pound note.

'Yeah, and that sounds great,' mock I. 'And then you look at the people who are actually saying it and they've been divorced about twelve times each. Rows aren't half as cathartic as dumping the rotten bastard, obviously.'

'Such cynicism in one so young!'

I swear, if my Dr Alibhai was on a menu in a posh Frog nosh joint, she'd be called *Jeune Truite Supérieure*.

'Not so cynical, but not so young, either.' I'm off. 'Old enough to see that cynicism is a sort of innocence, though.' But I tear myself with a quite determined effort off the teetering clifftop highway which leads irretrievably to Cliché City, and turn the beat around. 'Do you know what, Usha? I think there's such a thing as the *Final Row*. But – get this – it's not necessarily the *last* row a couple ever have. It usually isn't. But what it is, to all intents and purposes, is the row which marks the end of the affair, or the marriage, or whatever. Whether the two people involved know it or not – well, usually only one of them knows it. There'll be lots of good times and vows of love undying and great sex before the decree nisi – but that Final Row was the moment when the heart, because of something screamed or said or done, finally went AWOL. Once and for all.'

She's silent. She's thinking – or perhaps she's just being silent. 'And what does it feel like, this AWOL feeling?'

I think about it. 'Well – I guess you suddenly feel sort of about two stones lighter and ten years younger and sort of semi-detached: you're still *there*, in the house, in the flesh, but in reality you're already gone. Your heart moves into a sort of half-way house. On ice. You sort of go into an emotional chill cabinet. Ready for the next time. The *next love*.'

'And this is the way you feel?'

'No, I'm making it up for cheap thrills, aren't I? But seriously, Usha – I've felt this way before, with other people. But I never *dreamt* I'd feel it with Matt.'

'But you do?'

'I don't know.' I draw on my cigarette, burn my fingers, put it out. Out of mind. 'No. I don't want to know.'

But, as you do, we've fallen into some sort of domestic routine, twisted and bitterly dismaying as it may be.

A typical evening with the Addams Family will find little Nicole back at the drawing board screwing a very expensive French drawing pencil viciously around in a minute, exquisitely sharp pencil sharpener and wishing that said pencil was really her hubby's knob. Liza, the heartbeat of my bloodline, will be watching something to do with violence or death, or preferably violent death, on TV. A hard-hitting documentary on the latest serial killer or a stage-managed boxing bout, she ain't fussy.

And looka here, what's all this – it's Matthew, bless him, fiddling with his zoom lens in a manner which suggests that he could quite easily make himself blind in the process. He looks at me and I look away, icily I hope.

'What do heterosexual women like to do after sex?' I say innocently, still sharpening my nib.

'I don't know,' he says suspiciously, but intent on humouring me. 'What do heterosexual women like to do after sex?'

'*Come*.' I laugh; mirthlessly, I hope.

He looks away – and then he looks at Liza. This is nothing particularly new – he's looked at her before. Well, she's a *woman*, isn't she? Forget the fact that she's got a beard, three fine warts from which mustard and cress appear to be sprouting and that she smells like a dish-washing machine that has been left to bear its steaming bounty for a good three weeks of a long hot summer – hey, this brave boy's slept with *Bridget*, he ain't no wuss.

But somehow he's looking at her *differently* now; he's looking at her profile, if indeed three warts, a hooked shnozz and a hairy chin can be called a profile. You don't see that many cameo brooches of such ladies, do you? But he *is*, he's looking at her with real interest – almost *fascination*: her wiry, racked frame, her clenched fists, her hunched back as she leans forward in her chair muttering the immortal words, 'Mash 'is goolies, Yokozuma!' And what do you know? He lifts his camera quick as a zip, and he shoots her.

Liza turns, surprised. 'Whassat?'

He doesn't move. 'Say cheese, Leez!'

'Lize!' she cackles. Then her gums flash grotesquely – wouldn't you know, she's got her teeth out. ''Ard Cheddar!'

He snaps her again – this Devil-spawned, demonic, toothless crone's physical presence apparently holding all the allure of Christy's mouth, Cindy's eyes and Kate's endless doomed glory. 'Give it to me, pussycat!' And then they both burst out in gales of completely uninhibited, lip-synching laughter.

And guess who's the punchline again.

Well you won't believe this at first, but the long and the short of it is that little Nicola here's been hoisted by the short and curlies yet once more. Before you can say Veruschka, or in Liza's case verucca, Matthew's jumping about like a mad thing eight days a week snapping away at the malevolent old witch like she's God's gift to ground glass.

We're treated to stark, though hardly stylish, black and white eight-by-ten glossy studies of Liza eating (not for the weak stomach, these), Liza drinking (Guinness from the bottle, cider from the can, tea from the saucer – the usual panoply of urbane metropolitan poses), Liza watching grown men with silly names and shaven chests do their equal best to crush each other to death in this ringed, *fin de siècle*, extra-terrestrial Bedlam with bells (and smells) on we call satellite TV,

Liza winding bone-thin curlers hopefully through her snow-white, piteously thin hair – quite touching, really, this one, the doomed daily grind of a *bona fide* beast still attempting to turn itself into a big-haired beauty. Luckily we are spared Liza picking her nose – 'You kin pick yer friends, and you kin pick yer nose, but you can't pick yer friends' noses!' she is fond of gleefully cackling when caught in the act – and Liza sitting on the lavvy, studying the form in *WWF Weekly*, which my perve hubby was for some reason really up for.

So finally Matt's got a beezer set of twenty-four of these babies, the thickness of which he slaps down triumphantly on my drawing board beneath my nose one day, wearing a crocodile smile so broad you'd be forgiven for thinking that the glossies were his dick and that my customary domestic semi-sneer (which I habitually wear around my lord and master the way Oxo Katie wore Playtex Living Bras around hers) was actually a salivating snarl, dripping drool all over the mighty sceptre as a handy pre-coital lubricant. Well, it's *not*. We're *married*, must I keep reminding you?

'So?' I state rudely. It's the sort of thing a rude foreigner might say, or that you'd say to a rude foreigner. I've noticed this about people's behaviour when they're so-called romantically involved. Not only do most people – especially men – find it impossible for any sustained length of time (like five minutes) to treat the person they live with with one quarter of the common courtesy they'd show a stranger on the street, but pretty soon they even start talking to them as though they don't speak the language. Which they don't – the language of *love* that is.

Yes, class, I think we can safely say that the death of love is second to none in making the ex-object of adoration look *utterly* like a funny, duty-free foreigner – baffled, a stranger in Lonesome Town, wrongly believing you to be a resident of Love City Central who is somehow equipped to lead the way. Wearing weird clothes (how come you never noticed that sweater before?), not realising that their visa to your heart has run out well and good this time. You're the Immigration Squad and they're the unwanted wetback – Oi, you! Get back to where you came from! Coming over here, taking our hearts . . .

So I'm looking at Matthew as though he's asked me the way to somewhere deeply unfashionable, like a house party in West Kensington on a Saturday night, and I don't quite speak the lingo. When I know, of course, that I'm meant to be having forty fits over his cretinous eight-by-tens before shrieking: 'Oh, husband mine! You're an effing genius, you are! You've done my head in with your ability to press a little button and then trot down to Boots the Chemist with a roll of celluloid!' (He doesn't, of course, but anyway.) 'Thanks to you and *only* you – forget Avedon, Arbus, Bill Brandt – I now at last, after twenty-odd years of non-stop sneering, believe that, yes, *photography is an art form on a par with the painting of pictures and the composing of music*! Yes, if da Vinci was alive today he most likely wouldn't be painting the "Mona Lisa", but taking pictures of girl tennis players scratching their BTMs! And it stands to reason, then, that if Beethoven was alive today, he wouldn't sit around deafening himself with boring old symphonies – no, he'd be taking black and white glossies of men with huge breasts and even huger hair staring mournfully at naked babies as though they couldn't decide whether to kiss them, kill them or eat them whole in a club sandwich – heavy on the lettuce, hold the mayo!'

So: 'What d'you mean, "so"?' he pipes indignantly. 'Just *look* at it, will you? It's an *essay*. An essay in light and shade. *Chiaroscuro*. A memento in monochrome. The word made flesh.'

'Hardly,' I say maliciously. I peer at them, sneering. 'But if it was, just out of curiosity, what would this little essay, you being such a worthy successor to Mr Hazlitt and all that, be called, do you think? "In Praise of Involuntary Euthanasia" 's quite good, I think. Quite Swiftian.'

He sweeps up his bounty smugly. 'Temper, temper, my sweet. Other people besides yourself *are* allowed to *look* at the old bird, you know. The camera's not going to steal her *soul* or anything – she's not Anna Mae Wong.'

'No, she's not! Thank you, Matthew! Thank you for *noticing* that interesting little fact, at last!' I've got him now! 'Liza is not young, to put it mildly, and furthermore, she is *not* beautiful – not in the conventional, plastic sense,' I added quickly. Have you noticed that whenever we use the word 'plastic' about someone's looks, we actually mean 'better-looking than me'? As though you couldn't get ugly plastic or something! 'And I don't want people *laughing* at her!'

'Laughing at her!' he gibbers, pointing excitedly at his haul. Or rather his trawl. 'Who's laughing at her? *She's* laughing, Nic. At *us*.'

'OK.' I light a fag and have a think. One's considerably easier than the other these days, I don't suppose I have to tell you. 'What's your angle this time?'

'It's simple, really.' Well, he's definitely the man for the job then. He sits down beside me; I sidle away, Miss Muffet protecting her muff. He spreads out the photographs on my drawing board – which is the sort of visual-arts equivalent of that notorious Dirty Protest at the Maze Prison, if you want my honest opinion. 'Look at this study of Liza.'

I look. This is a really choice one, too. She's gurning in a somewhat unattractive, medieval manner at the unseen TV screen (which doubtless displays some sort of combat to the death) and she's got huge bits of crispy-crumb coating sticking in her beard. 'Bloody lovely,' I say sarkily. 'Wipes the floor with that boring old Mainbocher corset Polaroid, when you look at it closely.'

'Right. Yeah.' Stupid bastard. He's one of those humourless tossers who invariably say that sarcasm is the lowest form of wit, when of course not only could they never dream of *doing* it, but they wouldn't even *recognise* sarcasm if it came charging at them on horseback across a huge blasted heath waving a spiked ball on a chain and dishing out savage *bons mots* at the top of its voice. 'Now look at this – and then think about the last photograph you saw of an old bid – of a person of Liza's age.'

I snigger. 'Can't remember. Go on.'

'Well, they'd been beaten up, probably,' he says, all *caring*. 'Or they were on some tacky black and white poster advertising hypothermia or something. Whatever. But the point is, *they weren't enjoying themselves*! Like Liza always is! It's a whole new other concept, Nic – a whole new take on the ageing process! Let's face it, youth's been done to death –'

'Yes, darling, and mostly done by *you*.'

'– but *age*! It's like, "I've seen the future – and it's got cataracts!" I can just see the first big campaign now: BE OLD, BE FOOLISH – BUT BE HAPPY!' He hugs, literally *hugs* himself in delight. 'Think of it, Nic! You could use it to flog anything – from Guinness to life insurance!'

'Or indeed a dead horse,' I hiss before drawing myself up to my full height. 'Because excuse *me*! You're talking about flogging my *grandmother*, in case you hadn't noticed! As though she was one of your slaggy little model friends!' (Only better-looking and with nicer table manners. Me, I say nothing.)

He jumps off his perch and heads for the door. 'Who's flogging who? Don't worry, she'll get paid.'

'Yeah,' I shout after him. 'A four-pack of stout with one can missing, and half a packet of humbugs with the stripes licked off, if I know anything about *your* level of generosity to any human female over the age of eighteen!'

He stops at the door, spins on his heel – and dang me if he doesn't, as he twinkles at me, look almost lethal in his single-mindedness. For a minute I could fancy him myself if we weren't awfully wedded.

'Let's let Liza decide for herself, shall we?'

Chapter **Eleven**

You don't even need me to tell you what O Great Gurning One made of all this: the chance to earn her weight in pigs' feet, just for the usual daily round of gracious living – slurping from her saucer, picking her corns and flicking them into my Etruscan urns, urging naked wrestlers on to greater feats of slaughter than even they would normally contemplate – and having it captured in timeless eight-by-ten.

So now, gradually, little Nicola's days take on a new, richer pattern, i. bloody e. standing around a freezing loft from dawn till dusk watching Oh-no-it's-Grandma prancing around, in so far as her arthritis will allow, for the priapic lens of Matthew Miller. Remember that scene with Veruschka and David Hemmings from *Blow-Up*, the sexiest snapper scenario ever? Well, it's nothing like that, for a start. But try telling *them* that.

'More teeth, pussycat! Show me those teeth!'

Liza takes out her dentures and holds them towards him on the palm of her hand, grinning gummily.

'Brilliant!' He laughs, snapping her. 'You're a natural!'

'Oh for God's sake!' I walk away from them, towards my drawing board. *Back to the drawing board*, in fact. This horrible phrase, which means metaphorically that you've royally screwed something up, is what I spend my life literally doing. This just can't be a coincidence, can it? What proportion of the population do you think spend their life actually doing this, do you think? It's a bloody black joke, if you ask me, played on me by that bastard Life. *Back to the drawing board, Nicola!*

'Don't thee blaspheme, young lady!' Liza warns, the muse turning moral guardian for a moment, 'or I'll wash thy mouth out with carbolic, I will!' She would, too, malign old biddy.

'*Please*, darling.' Matt changes his dinky job for some big black beast – sort of what I did with him and Remi in reverse, Sound of Hollow Laughter! – without even looking at me. '*Don't* upset the talent. Don't you have a nice drawing to do or something?'

'Don't you *dare* treat me like a child!' I hiss.

He looks up now, and looks right into me. For the first time, it's not sexy. 'Then stop doing that to Liza.'

'I was so mad, Dr Alibhai, when he said that. You can't *imagine* how mad I was. *Him!* Telling *me* how to treat my own flesh and blood!'

'Oh, I can. I can well imagine.'

Something soft in her voice makes me stop and think of her as a human being for a second. Instead of a sounding board crossed with a sex object. 'It's either feast or famine, isn't it, doctor?' I say seductively (I hope). 'Feast or famine – when it comes to *love*.'

'Oh, I don't know about that, Nicole,' she says,

about as responsive as a kipper gone cold. 'I really don't. With you, I imagine that it's either feast or finger buffet. Surf or turf. Surf *and* turf. Or worse.'

So she's not having any, is she? I can live with that. One never loses an ally; one merely gains an audience.

So I switch to Show-Off mode: 'But then, doctor, I had this brilliant idea. Well, it was bad as well as brilliant –'

'Go on.'

'But – and I ask you this in all sincerity – was it really any more bad than what *he* was doing? Which was, basically, *stealing my own grandmother from me*? *From under my nose*? (Which makes it worse, somehow.) No! – how could it be? And they *do* say all's fair in love and war . . .'

'*Who* do, Nicole?' Pedantic cow.

'Well, unprincipled slags in general and people who are about to stitch someone up, usually their best friend or a blood relation, I suppose. But you know what I mean –'

'I most certainly do.'

'So anyway, what I did was waited until Liza went on one of her foraging trips to the chippy one day, and then the minute I heard her key in the door I picked up the phone . . .'

'Hello? Yes. Yes, she does live here. To whom am I addressing, please?' Hell. Got *that* bit wrong. Not that *she'll* notice.

I'll give you a day in Liza's life, if you can call it a life. At approximately five a.m., when Matthew (an occasional visitor to his home, to give him credit where it's due) and I are falling into an unrefreshing sleep after either a bout of fucking that feels like fighting or fighting that feels like fucking, Liza will greet the new day with a Morning Has Broken chorus of heaving, belching and wind-breaking that might find you forgiven for thinking that she had the entire crew-chorus of the Volga Boatmen in there with her.

Then, as Matthew and I regard each other with that same shell-shocked expression of original sin and thoroughly unoriginal remorse with which I used to greet each new morning's labour over the porcelain, we hear the clean, lean, human machine that is Liza Sharp, twentieth-century Titan, crank slowly into life. That creaking, cursing arising from her fetid bed of sin, or at least Deep Heat (which is surely something Dante would have come up with had he been a mad pharmacist; Burning Hell in a handy-sized tube), the shuffling of the becorned, beslippered feet, slippers that are by now slippers in name only, the heels ground down by life, the toes worn away by strife or at least the least benign, most block-busting bunions ever seen outside a *Manga* comic. These truly are the bunions that could eat Berlin Undivided – but often when I think about them, these bunions bring tears to my eyes as though they were my very own and some lout in steel-capped shoes had stepped on them. Because the bunions that disfigure her feet will one day disfigure mine. We're all sleepwalking towards them, bunions, even as we high-step it to the ball in Kurt Geiger's finest fuck-me sling-back sandals. We may think we're dancing towards *bona fide* belle-of-the-balldom, but we're really just prancing towards Bunion Hell.

So Liza starts her day shuffling across the loft floor and making it sound like she's at last shuffling off this mortal coil, and I start the day in tears, or at least in Stolly-and-Slimline leakage from the approximate watermark. And usually, when I'm depressed, which must easily be eighty per cent of my waking hours these days, I seek to escape the landlocked numbness of life with one brief shining explosion of ecstasy. But as there's not much of that about these days, I tend to settle for sex with my husband.

'Make love to me!' I murmur, with Liza safely locked in the lavatory.

He generally looks at me blankly. 'Do what? Oh, right.'

He mounts me and slides in like a greased speculum, but without all that teeming emotion. I'm like a bloody modern theatre designed for disabled groupies, me: Access All Areas. What I've basically got is the opposite of a lubrication problem, when all's said and done; I'd be ready for it with the very bailiff who came to evict me from hearth and home. With the assassin who pulled the trigger. *With the man who married me.*

He makes me come, coldly, looking at me sideways out of the corner of his eyes as he moves slowly and steadily on top of me, as though I'm about to pull a fast one and turn into Michael Jackson – 'Ha ha, *fooled you*! Made you fuck a black man!' – and then he invariably asks, 'Are you finished?'

'Yes,' I pant.

He starts to move again, pushing towards his climax, and if I'm really up for it I can slip in another one of my own that leaves him somewhat surprised and resentful towards my capacity for sexual ecstasy even with someone I actually wouldn't cross the road to expectorate into the mouth of if he was dying of thirst. As a parting shot: 'I love you!' I murmur as he pulls none too gently out of me, and I can really get off on his bafflement at this time in the morning. I also, into the bargain, get a distinct and exquisite pain from registering that, yet again, he doesn't say, 'I love you' back.

Well, Liza will be out of the lavatory by now, and Matthew's out of me, so everyone's shot their wad for the a.m. It's a.m., therefore I am! Let the revels begin! Which means Liza puts the kettle on and Matthew puts his skates on, all the better to spend a full working day shooting off in Siobhan's face – sorry, did I say that? Shooting off *rolls of film* of Siobhan's face, was what I meant to say.

Making tea which she won't drink to refresh a brain which won't think but which sort of sits there in her cranial cavity like a teabag suspended in lukewarm water will easily fill a wholesome and productive morning for Granny, but around noon she's going to get peckish and shove off for a saveloy or two to bridge that penis-sized gap in her digestive system (which would appear to be the only place such a gap ever existed). And it's on her snuffly and triumphant return from the chippy that she just, only *just* mind you, happens to catch her little Nicola on the telephone.

'I'm addressing who? Oh!' I do a little disco-bunny jump-back, supposed to indicate a startled fawn, giving Liza the full monty as she comes through the door. But she's found something up her nose and is examining it with all the fervid wonder of Oppenheimer regarding the first split atom. 'From the *Department of Health and Social Security*? Oh! Yes!'

Well, I've got her now. '*The Social?*' she stage-whispers, drawing back against the wall, clutching her sweating saveloys to her black old heart. 'Nic'la! Tell 'em! Tell 'em I'm not living 'ere, pet!'

I make a not-now-Gran face, shaking my head ferociously and placing my finger to my lips in a woe-betide-you gesture (isn't it weird how only teachers ever actually *say*, 'Woe betide you'? Do they teach them it at training college or something?) before turning my back on her to hide my smile of triumph. My, what big *eyes* you've got, Grandma! And what a big *damp patch* seems to be appearing on your old camel-coloured cloth coat! All the better to *sign your own death warrant with*!

'Well, yes – sir – she *does* live here, actually.' I turn and look at her. She's clawing at the air in this non-specific supplicating gesture, which I study with some interest. Isn't it great, sometimes, being modern and not caring about people and stuff?

'And she's done *what*?' Crucial – now she's genuflecting, the old fraud. Except for the minute detail that, not being a Roman Catholic, she's never genuflected in her life before. So that instead of looking like some dead classy doomed gesture from a Muriel Spark novel it looks like some obscene version of 'The Hokey-Cokey' instead. She's starting from the *bottom*, would you believe, so that the Sign of the Cross comes out instead like some lewd sexual insinuation. 'Well, yes – sir –' (chuck in a few unspecified 'sir's just to get the wind all the way up her – can't hurt, can it?) 'yes, yes, I *did* know that *that* was against the law.' (Law! Just the very word makes her eyes stand out on stalks.

Literally. Just *think* of all the crimes, petty or otherwise, the old fraud must have committed during her long and awful life. I'm practically doing society a favour here.)

'Oh – no, *really*, sir?' Liza's turning sort of blue now, sort of Militia; I'd better bring it down a few notches. 'But surely – not *prison* . . .'

There. I'd done it again. I'd made a beast of myself, probably to escape for a minute the pain of being human, but that's not the point. I couldn't resist it, and now my granny, the love of my life, the only living being on this rotten planet I would go through hell, high water or South London after seven o'clock at night for, was expiring on the floor before me. And was I happy? Was I hell. I was snow-blind with elation. Because, for the first time since I'd rescued her from a fate worse than daytime TV, she needed me. Actually *needed* me. I was the only one who could save her. That I was the only one who'd put her in her nightmarish situation in the first place was neither here nor there. It was nit-picking, to be blunt.

'But, sir, she has always, *always* in the past been such a law-abiding old lady. I really do feel, though I don't want to name names – yes, yes, absolutely – that her only true crime on this occasion' – we'll draw a veil over that sequence of shimmering Sixties Saturdays when she played a surgical-stockinged, Guinness-guzzling Charles Manson to her very own Family of brainwashed lost boys and girls just for once, shall we? – 'was perhaps being too trustful – too easily led, if you know what I mean.' I laugh maddeningly with my imaginary ally. 'As they are, at that age.'

I eye my passion dispassionately as she squints up at

me from the floor. And, cunning old chiseller that she is, she *knows* she's home free.

'Yes, sir . . . I *do* understand now that what has been taking place Under My Roof is a grave offence, under the circumstances. And I *do* see why prison is the usual punishment. Yes, exactly . . . it's not about retribution, is it? Yes. Yes. *Exactly*. It's about fair shares for all. Making sure dog doesn't eat dog – even if he *is* a sausage dog and looks sort of tasty and you're a Great Dane and you feel sort of peckish.' I'm losing it now, I know, irretrievably tempted by stage centre, even if it is a mirage, which is well and truly *tragic* – but on the other hand, what the hell. Better wind it up, though – while we're a winner!

'Sir, I cannot – literally *cannot* – express to you my gratitude for showing such clemency in this instance. Oh! The very person we've just been discussing has literally this minute walked through the door! Would you like a word with her?'

Smiling, I hold the instrument of torture out to Liza, who immediately goes into St Vitus Dance mode, thrashing about from her lowly perch and giving it a lot of the Happy Eater finger-to-mouth dumb show (what *happened* suddenly when they took Mr Happy Eater's finger out of the logo, do you think? Was it just like some day some type in the art department woke up and realised the thing that we'd all been sniggering over for aeons, which was that Mr Happy Eater looked for all the world as though he was on the totally ecstatic verge of making himself throw up?) which is presumably supposed to indicate that she doesn't want to talk to anyone right now. Hey, I can work with that.

I bring the receiver back to my mouth. 'I'm *so* sorry, sir, but Grandma appears to have been caught short on this occasion. Yes – bless. Very well – I will be *sure* to tell her. And just one more thing, if I may – if you *should* see the magistrate who was scheduled to pass sentence, please emphasise in the strongest possible terms that she *is* a very law-abiding senior citizen, on the whole. What I feel about this whole situation – and you'll excuse me if I bang on a bit, because it's a particular hobby-horse of mine –' and here I giggle garishly, girlishly, just ishly really, it's that sickening, 'is that, when it comes down to it, we as a society bend over backwards – *literally* – to absolve young people of any misdemeanour, no matter how massive, just because they're allegedly not in their right minds, or depressed, or poor, or subject to peer-group pressure! But I ask you, sir, in all good faith – how many of our *old* folk aren't out of their minds, or depressed, or subject to the *savage* peer-group pressure you'll find at any given daycare centre? Let alone poor!'

I give it some Coventry here to make it sound like the phantom snooper on the other end of the line is making a contribution to the debate. I nod earnestly, like I'm listening and taking notice of someone else's opinions or whatever it is people do. 'Exactly, sir. *Exactamente!* And do our old folk get sent on *QE2* cruises as a reward for flagrantly flouting the laws of our land? Do they many!' More Coventry-cackle from me before I wind it up by nodding like a car-dog on coke for half a minute and then replacing the phone with a flourish.

I look stonily down at Liza, who with the callous lack of gratitude and God-fearingness so typical of her age and class has completely recovered her composure now she knows she's off the hook and the Social won't be sending a customised, commode-toting paddy-wagon round to carry her off in. 'Well. Let's hope they don't follow *that* phone call up, or this household can add perjury to its list of crimes.'

'Wass talking about, wench?' She's scrabbling to her feet and dusting herself down. *That's* a laugh. Dusting herself down! – she's *made* of dust. She'd *disappear* if she dusted herself down successfully.

'Law-abiding old lady. Trusting. Easily led. You're about as easily led as a rhino wearing roller-blades!'

She cackles. 'What they want with me down the Social, anyway? I 'aven't done nuffin'.'

I follow her into our gracious living space. She immediately renders it a flophouse – just by standing there, radiating. She's sort of Princess Grace in reverse. They say that Grace Kelly was a princess from the day she was born. I can't believe that Liza didn't slip into this world picking her nose, sucking a humbug and smelling of toilets. 'Oh, but you have, Gran! Well, not *you*, but Matthew. Taking those photographs of you –'

'There weren't nothing wrong with them pictures! I kept me bloomers on!' She scuttles into the kitchen area; she's 'Metamorphosis' in reverse, a black beetle who woke up one morning and found to his horror that he was Liza Sharp.

'Yes, I *know*, love.' I'm doing my Claire Rayner bit here. I attempt to put my arms around her as she stands up from peering into the fridge; she ejaculates a can of Guinness all down the front of my Ghost. I hold my tongue and my temper, or rather they hold each other back, in the manner of bar-room brawlers. 'But you were still drawing your old-age pension, weren't you? You didn't tell the people at the Post Office that you had a new job, did you?'

'What job?' More Guinness goes down her outside than her inside. She doesn't seem to notice the difference.

'As a . . . photographic model.' Don't all laugh at once.

'Nic'la!' Liza slams down her can. There is real panic in her voice. 'Nic! I din' do nuffin' wrong! I din' take no money! Not yet! Young Matt was gonna sell 'em first, to the adverts! Then I'd get my cut. Please . . .'

'Are you *sure* you never took a penny?' I know; just call me Witchfinder General.

'Positive! Cross my 'eart!' She does something obscene with her gnarled old nipples. 'Just a couple a Guinnesses, I swear!'

'Guinnesses . . . mmm . . .' I pretend to think about it. 'I *suppose* that that could be seen as a legitimate gift. Not bribery . . .'

'Bribery! Bribery and corruption? I never did! I never *would*!' She makes a face implying that Mother Teresa is the mother of all streetwalkers, panhandlers and payola merchants compared to her, Liza Sharp.

I figure she's had enough. So I keep her dangling for a nanosecond longer and then I say in this soft, wheedly voice: 'Listen, Gran. I don't think it's too late. Not quite. But you *must* stop posing for Matt. *Right now*.'

'But 'e's not 'ere!' She looks around her in terror.

I've well and truly put the frighteners on her. She can't *wait* to stop.

'No. But he will be soon. And then you must tell him *as soon as possible* that he cannot use the photographs he's already taken in any way, shape or form whatsoever.'

She nods frantically. 'Right you are.'

'But on the other hand,' I smarm silkily, 'you musn't tell him *why* you've changed your mind. Because he'll just feed you a load of Optrex about how he can make it all right with the Social – and you know how easily led you are, Gran. He's money-mad, that man.'

Liza nods solemnly. 'The root of all evil, money.'

No, dear – that's my husband's penis, bless its scabby little helmet. 'Yup – and what Matthew doesn't know about evil roots really isn't worth knowing.'

I can see the sweet old thing trying to work this out in her poor fuddled brain, bless her – evil roots? Carrots, swedes, turnips? Eventually she gives it up as a bad job. 'So then I'll be all right, will I? With the Social?'

I grab my coat from the back of the sofa and pull it on with the sort of resolve that implies I'm about to go out and overturn a couple of democratically elected governments before lunch. 'Tell you what, Gran. I'm going round there right now. I'll sort things out for you, if it's the last thing I do. I'll make everything all right.'

'Oh, Nic-Nic!'

Liza flies at me like a demon, like she used to do when I was twelve years old. Except this time it's not to clout me, but to cling to me as though she will never let me go. Well, *yes*; I can live with that.

I put my arms around her and close my eyes. I feel her tremble with fear and relief as I hold her close. And I reflect, luxuriously, that this is about as perfect as life gets. When you're a grown-up.

Dr Alibhai snorts. 'So she thinks you're –'

'At the DHSS, yeah.' I snigger and select a little tool from my Tweezerman kit. Dr Alibhai lets me do my manicure on the couch now. Because I'm her special ladeee. And because I was driving her out of her tiny Chinese mind with my twitchiness. I'm used to doing five things at once, see. Especially when I'm – heh heh – horizontal. 'On my knees, begging for them not to send the Black Maria round to take her away. Ha ha.' I push at my cuticles. It hurts, in a searing, sexual sort of way. 'Why is it that "Black Maria" isn't spelt like Mariah Carey, d'you think? Rather than Maria Callas. Because it *sounds* like Mariah Carey. Isn't that weird?'

'*You're* weird.'

I smile, smugly. I can't help it. I'm *indestructible*, like in the Spandau Ballet song.

'Please, doctor. Don't make value judgements. Especially not in the mental health line.'

'OK. Not weird.'

I stretch and purr.

'*Warped.*'

Chapter **Twelve**

So after my quota of quality time with my shrink – which must be the only quality time anyone ever really gets with anyone these days; they can't walk out the door if you're paying them to stay put, after all – I go off to get blitzed with Zoë. We end up, don't you just know it, back at hers, drinking vodka, listening to yet *more* maudlin black broads singing as if their big old hearts were fit to break – and talking about men and absorbency.

I don't know why this is, but girls' nights out in my set always end up in vapid nattering about men and absorbency these days. But there was a time, back in our raging twenties, when we'd sit up all night talking about our careers and politics and what sign we were. Now it's men and absorbency. Saps and sanitary protection – how thick they are. Really, is that any life for a dog?

And the funny thing is, *I don't think we really care about men and absorbency any more.* I think we cared more about them in our twenties, when it didn't occur to us to talk about them more than twice a year. I think now that we're in our thirties, we're really tired and pissed off and we couldn't give a damn about getting or keeping our man out of anything more than some ridiculous, over-lasting teenage sense of competition; let alone embarrassing leakage. These days we'd just laugh.

And our new-found self-contained desireless state makes us, in the wee small hours of the morning, feel frightened that we're becoming dried-up sexless old sticks like we thought (hoped? prayed?) our mothers were. (Female sexual responsiveness being signified, you'll note, by being a needful bag of hormones. Oh, *really*? Who wrote *that* textbook?) And in denial, for each other's benefit – because women's best-kept secret is that we do *everything* for other women's eyes, from dressing to dancing to, let's face it, *fucking*; eventually this strikes us as a bit of an effort, and we simply cut out the middle man and go gay – we do this terrible female-impersonator thing whenever two or more of us are gathered in his name. All the huge-black-drag-queen stuff: Mah *man*! *Girl*friend! Miss *Thang*! Keep your *hands* off of mah *man*, *girlfriend*! Get with the *programme*! *Ooo-eee*! Get *her*!

And it's just sad, and sorry, and insulting. Without wishing to insult huge black drag queens, I really don't think that Emily Wilding Davison chucked herself under a racehorse so that we could disport ourselves in this way, I really don't. Hey, I'm not suggesting that huge black drag queens throw themselves under racehorses, either – they got their own problems. But why can't we both just do what we do best?

So after Zoë and I have exhausted both ourselves and the possibilities inherent in flinging oneself around to De'Lacey records and screeching at the tops of our voices about our *mahhhn*, we fall to the floor and to talking in a maudlin manner about our men.

'The trouble with men,' La Zo pronounces, slopping Stolly on to the floorboards, but mis-aiming and spilling a few drops into my glass, 'is that we don't *want* them but we *need* them.'

'I thought the trouble was that we don't *need* them but we do *want* them.' I'm always one to put the radical view.

'Nah . . . no . . . it's like . . . the plug needs the electricity. The plug doesn't *want* the electricity – but it needs it . . .'

I realise then that Zoë is so drunk that she isn't even going to be fun any more, and Zoë can be fun in her sleep as a rule. It's weird with drinking. If you're matching someone drink for drink, there's not an iota of doubt in your mind whatsoever that they're the wittiest, sharpest company the world could ever hold without splitting its sides laughing. If you should stumble and fall behind in the imbibing stakes, however, suddenly you find that Oscar Wilde's been wheeled out on a trolley while your back was turned topping up their glass and Muma the Dog-Faced Boy is doing Laffs Duty for him instead.

Muma will later be joined by his talkative friends Coco the Clown, Donald the Duck and Nellie the Natural (Who Only Comes Out When the Moon is Full) for a four-way Family Favourites selection of stimulating debates on such subjects as men, religion and politics, i.e. – and get your notebooks ready, class, for you will never have heard the like of these pearls before – 'Can't live with 'em, can't live without 'em,' 'They've been responsible for more wars than anything else – but Jesus was cool' and 'They're all the same!' Interestingly, these three phrases are completely interchangeable.

So I throw my woes and my lipstick into my Dolce & Gabbana rucksack, kiss Zoë chastely on the brow, say, 'I may be gone for some time' and hightail it home.

Liza and Matt are sitting at opposite ends of the sofa, with faces on them like Christmas in Kuwait. I know I'm a bitch. But I'm also a bit drunk, which excuses it. I dance into the middle of the room and throw out my arms, knees slightly bent to one side, in the classic Broadway finale pose, and yell:

'IS EVERYBODY HAPPEEE?'

A lot can happen in twenty-four hours. A revolution. A revelation. Markets and empires and idols may fall. And a noble, accomplished, serenely beautiful woman living in a Docklands dream home may discover a cache of glossy eight-by-twelves depicting a *bona fide* boner-riding teenage whore minus her clothing. When this happens, she may quite understandably suspect that every roll of used film on the premises contains similar obscene images. And she may quite reasonably tear open all of her husband's – Mr Scum, by name – many cameras in search of said filth. In order that she may destroy it and make the world a better, safer place for future generations.

'There!' Another one hits the dust – quite literally, as the floor of our glorified hutch is now a veritable smorgasbord of dustballs, due to the simple fact that *I'm too bloody depressed to do housework these days* (well, it's as good an excuse as any) – as I dance away behind the sofa, on which sits Liza soaking up a soap. She looks uncomfortably like a child trying not to hear its parents rowing, but I am righteously angry and it's too late to stop now. 'Yet another boring, bog-standard set of snaps of your darling Siobhan looking as though butter wouldn't melt in any given orifice which the world has been spared!'

Matt makes a grab at me and goes A over T across the sofa, falling on Liza. She pinches him viciously in the midriff and squirms away. 'You crazy bitch!' She pinches him again, in the nut region. 'Ow! *Not you!*' He comes round the sofa after me. 'That roll was worth thousands of pounds!'

'Well, I warned you that Siobhan was going to be the most expensive roll of your life, didn't I?' I throw yet another Kodak tickertape at the all-coming, – seeing, – conquering hero. 'Go and take some more, why don't you? Why not go all the effing way and have her fondling a frigging cucumber or something equally subtle? Then you can cut out the media middle man and sell them off a barrow in Soho yourself!'

'Those pictures were nothing to do with sex!' He grabs me by the wrist and we tussle over the camera.

'THEN WHY WASN'T SHE WEARING ANY FUCKING CLOTHES!' I scream at the top of my voice.

'Because she was under a waterfall, for the love of Mike –'

'*No!*' I crow triumphantly, having nailed the booby at last. 'No! *For the love of Matt!*'

'– under a waterfall, communing with Nature! She can hardly commune with Nature wearing a twinset and pearls, can she?'

'Why not? The Queen does!'

'The Queen isn't seventeen years old and physically perfect, is she? If she was, perhaps she'd strip off to go horse-riding, too!'

I lunge at him, pure with fury. 'Right! You're a dead man!'

'Bloody 'ell!' Liza stands up suddenly; past her, on the TV screen, I see a young couple fighting, and for a moment I think it's some horrible magic mirror reflecting us as the emotional midgets we all become when we indulge in this endless marital combat. 'Willst thee two put a sock in it for five minutes? It's the moment of truth on *EastEnders* – the blonde wench 'as just cottoned on that 'er 'usband's bin doin' somethin' disgustin' with a young tart!'

I hit Mr Scum around the head for luck, and throw the final roll of film at him. 'Really? She's not the only one!' And then I run into the toilet and lock the door, leaning against it panting. That's the trouble with this funky loft-living thing: if you ever need to make a dramatic exit, you're head-first down the bog.

Boy Wonder's banging on the door. 'Nicole! Open that door and come out of there and let's get this thing settled once and for all!'

'Come out?' I shout. 'Why should I? I've got everything I need in here! A toilet, a bidet, running water, a healthy supply of reading materials! Just let me have the portable telly and I'll live in here from now on! And you can move in with Miss Physically Perfect 1999!'

'At least she doesn't think that oral sex means talking about it instead of doing it!'

I looked down the toilet in fury, and I literally saw

red. I saw the red water churning, and I thought of the abortions I'd had, to keep my figure, to keep that *pig*. Not that it had bloody worked on either front, had it?

I unlock the door and yank it open and wailing like a banshee I throw myself at my lawfully wedded deadly enemy. He runs back to the sofa and we dodge and weave around it once more. I love my life. I really do.

'This is a bloody nightmare!' And Liza's on her feet again, totally getting into the spirit of the evening. 'Barrow Gurney 'ould be better than this! At least you could watch the telly there! If a woman oo's bin through two world wars and the decimal money can't watch the bleeding box when she feels like it, what can she do?' She stomps to the door. 'I'm off!'

'Graaan!' My voice is a babyish wail. 'Where're you *going*?'

She's throwing things into her string bag, which she had long before they were retro. Teeth, Everton mints, Guinness, the new WWF magazine. Your basics. She doesn't even look at me. 'Mick's place. Anything's got to be better than this *Carry On* caper.'

The door slams behind her and I turn to Matt, my voice trembling. 'You bastard. See what you've done now. Driven my own grandmother out into the cold.'

'It's July,' he points out pointlessly.

'It's never going to be July for us again, Matthew,' I decide, choking on my tears. 'It's going to be always winter and never Christmas.' I blur my way into the kitchen and start banging Daliesque pots and pans around. They're all melting. Like my life.

'Nic . . .' Mr Scum has followed me, and is lathering up the soft soap ready for application, judging by his voice. 'Come on. We've always been a good team. Haven't we?'

I've been here before, I'm sure of that. Yes, take a look over there – there's my little flag planted on a mound that commemorates the terminations I had because Mr Scum decided that we were 'a good team' who would suffer irretrievably from any addition. Two's company, three's a crowd, that's Matthew's view of marriage – unless the third is seventeen, no relation and physically perfect, of course. I wish I *had* had those children. They'd be just the age now for me to give them Creme Eggs and wheedle, 'Who do you love best? Mummy or Daddy? *Because Mummy loves you best!*' That and hold the child in front of me when Matt and I fight, and make it *see* what an evil fuck its father is.

'Only horses work in teams,' I shouted above the racket I was making with the pots and pans, 'horses and football players. Though considering the number of women you've shagged since we've been married, a football team is actually quite a good analogy.'

'You're impossible! Do you know that?' He swings me round roughly. And I want to cry, because it's not even sexy any more, being treated rough. It's just another variation on treading water in a shallow, sad marriage. 'You are literally impossible to live with.' He releases me. 'What is it *this* time? Got the curse?'

'Yes.' I put my hands in the sink and hang my head. Portrait of the Lawful Wedded State, *circa* any time at all. 'It's called marriage.'

'Well, Usha, after a decent interval he stormed out. I went at his favourite tapes with a pair of nail scissors and then passed out with last rites of Stolly. He came back next morning staggering under the weight of much bullshit and Casablanca lilies, woke me up and we did the usual.' I sniff a bit. 'The same old sad minuet of a marriage so far on the rocks that the open sea is just a distant memory.' I yawn. 'It's weird about sex. At one time I would have crawled across half a mile of broken glass just to put myself on the end of Matthew's dick. Now I keep wondering if I could call my mum and get her to write me a note. Like at school, when you want to get off Games.' I twirl my hair round my finger. I bet Siobhan's strand would have stayed in a shiny, sexy ringlet. Mine doesn't. 'Except I want to get off getting off.'

Dr Alibhai smiles. I call it 'Symphony in Satin and Enamel'. 'And was your grandmother party to all this hullabaloo and what-have-you?'

'No way! She slept over at that little bitch's hovel. She's done it before. Turned up very bright-eyed and bushy-tailed the next morning, too.' I turn on my stomach on her couch, which probably isn't kosher. But hell, neither am I. And it does show me off to my best advantage. 'But you haven't heard the end of it yet – or the worst. When we were in bed, Matt asked me to do a really *horrible* thing. Something I did ages ago for him, when I was really young, and I swore I'd never do again.'

She looks at me, dead serious. Well, I suppose that's ninety-five per cent of her job requirement really, isn't it? 'Was it something . . . sexual?'

'Nothing that clean.' I take a deep breath. 'He asked me to . . . have a *dinner party*, doctor! For *eight people*!'

She laughs with relief. Her laugh is like bells, and I want to jump out the window and just cling to their pealing silver lifebelt, swinging high over the city. Steady on. 'Is that so bad?'

I sit up, unbearably agitated. 'Yes! For a start, I can't cook! But even supposing I get the wretched thing catered, or I get Andrew, my friend the cook, to do it for me – I still have to act the hostess, don't I?' I shift on to my back again, moaning. 'And believe me, I'm *not* the hostess with the mostest, I'm the beastess with the leastest.'

She shakes her head and smiles. 'Oh, Nicole . . .'

'I know it sounds pathetic. But I just can't do it, even if someone else cooks. *Because I'd still have to be the one in charge. I'd have to be the grown-up.* And I still can't begin to tell you how much the idea of being one of those people frightens me.'

I look at her lovely, uncomprehending face. 'I'm sorry, doctor, but you can't possibly understand. Because *you're* such a grown-up. It's being Asian, I suppose . . . you sort of grow up sooner, don't you . . .'

'Oh, *yes.*' She folds her long hands in her lap. 'I learnt the womanly skills at my mother's silken knee. By the age of nine I could prepare a twelve-course feast fit for a Mogul king. And still get my homework done.'

'You see? You're so lucky, how you –'

She smiles broadly, the bitch.

'Oh, you're *joking.*' I feel somehow sadly diminished by the knowledge that my Dr Alibhai actually couldn't present me with a twelve-course Mogul feast if the need arose. 'Well, maybe I am being a bit of a saddo.' She raises an eyebrow, like 'Well, *yes.*' 'But it's not just *any* eight people he wants me to entertain with knobs on. One's Siobhan, would you believe it – "so you two can bury the hatchet once and for all". I'm not going to be so obvious, Usha, as to tell you I'd like to bury it in the Creature's silicone tits and call it performance art. Then there's Jonh With an H on the End, the merry dyslexic. And a pair of old cobblers – I'm not joking, they're these ancient but relentlessly trendy shoemakers. The fashion editor of a "crucial", or is it chronic, magazine. And last but not least, there's the character who books the photographers for – well, I won't say what magazine it is but if you're booked for a cover you're made for life, this life *and* all the reincarnations. You don't even have to get out of a supermodel's bed for less than £10,000 a day, *that's* for sure.'

Something occurs to me; anyone under the age of fourteen might call it a 'joke', if they were in a singularly merciful mood. 'What's the difference between Christy Turlington and Siobhan?'

She smiles like a Saturday girl. 'Give in.'

'Christy Turlington won't get out of bed for less than £10,000 and Siobhan won't get into bed for less than a tenner.'

She smiles, bless her! She doesn't want to, but she does! There *is* a god! 'It was Linda Evangelista, actually.' She shuffles her papers importantly. Hell, she *is* important. Just about the most important girl I know. 'And how will your grandmother deal with this proposed and traumatic dinner party?'

'Well, my dear husband, naturally, believes that any blood relation of mine must be so lacking in couth that they'd probably put their feet on the table and start picking – if not flicking – their corns somewhere between the starter and the entrée. So she's going to be shipped off to Michaela's for the night.'

'Will she mind? Being so obviously rejected like that?'

'Mind it! You're joking, aren't you? I told you, it's her second home these days. Michaela Kemp, as you might have guessed, comes from a long and particularly malevolent line of Haggerston hagglers and pearly pugilists. Half the family were boxers; the other half were wrestlers – and that's just the women. Of course, they think Gran's a caution because she's *au fait* with the name and form of every brute to have knocked someone stupid over the past fifty years.' I laugh, and a half. 'And of course *she's* in seventh heaven, to be staying somewhere where they've got a proper "lounge".' I smirk; it doesn't work. 'Three-piece suites and one-piece brains, doctor. That's what they've got.'

'Yes.' She blinks rapidly. 'What does that . . . *mean*, exactly?'

I shrug. 'Search me. But it sounds good.'

Chapter **Thirteen**

So eight days later I'm dressed up to the nines and feeling like a zero, with my foot in my mouth and my hands in a casserole, tearing up a chicken as though my life or Matthew's soprano depended on it. I'm *out*, to put it mildly: out of luck, out of sorts and out of bay leaves. And Lord Muck's luck is in, because against all the odds and protestations he's got an unpaid domestic slave sweating over a pot for him. Pot luck – but not for me.

Over in her usual chair – which by now actually *reeks* of her, and which I expect any day now to burp, amble over to the fridge and pull itself out a Guinness – the Dowager Lady Muck is sitting in her hat and coat with her shopping bag at her feet, watching *The Bill*. It's that time of night when *The Bill* comes on. But isn't it always?

Mr Scum, a.k.a. Lord Muck, comes up behind me. I know immediately he's in one of those home-is-my-harem/king-of-all-I-survey moods. When aren't they, really? But they're *especially* like it when they see a woman in a kitchen, with her hands in the sink or her brain in the Magimix. Then they get all my-woman mafioso macho. They think it's smart to come up behind you and suggest rear-entry sex. They wouldn't think it a bit smart or a bit clever to suggest rear – entry sex over a cooker if they knew that the image flashing through your mind at that white-hot moment of orgasm is not his hard, thrusting dick plunging in and out of you like a crazed, state-of-the-art piston but a massive saucepan full of boiling water being poured all over said crazed state-of-the-art piston by the worm who has finally turned, the dog who has finally barked and the bitch who finally decides that all doggy-style sex does for her is make her feel like a hole with a leg at each corner. Just try it, Mr Scum!

He puts his arms around my waist, but chastely – luckily for him – and sniffs. He looks like the Bisto Kids' grandad. 'Something smells good.'

'Yes, well, it certainly isn't your breath.'

He releases me, like he was never really interested in getting a gratis grope. 'Very funny.' He whispers: 'When's Madame Defarge off?'

'As soon as she's wound back her new video to take to the Kemps'. Ali versus Liston. Got it for her this morning. She's watched it three times already.'

Matthew looks at her, dead dry and amused. 'Amazing, isn't it? A lifetime of misery and struggle, and all she's interested in is watching two people turn each other into twelve tins of cat food.'

'Well, she certainly came to the right place.' I brush past him with the casserole dish. 'Mind your feet. I can tell you've only just combed them.'

He sighs, following me. 'Nic. *Please* be sweet tonight. You know how important this thing is to me.' He peers into the dish. 'What's that?'

'*Coq au vin*. What else, considering Siobhan's coming?'

'But Jonh's a lacto-ovo vegetarian!'

'Then let him go and suck a chicken's teat!'

'I mean it, Nicole. This night could be the start of something big for both of us.'

I have to laugh at his sheer gall. When was the last time *anything* was ever 'big' for both of us at once? Like in the same room at the same time? Especially his dick, if we're going to be crude about it. 'What do you mean, "us", white man? I don't have any interest in impressing your pals!'

'Don't you?' He swings me round to face him. 'Don't you really, Nic? Or didn't I tell you that Gavin's boyfriend books all the mag's illustrators and artists, too? And that he particularly asked Gav to check you out this evening? I didn't tell you that?' He laughs softly. 'Silly me.'

I stand back and look at him. I might well look hungry. To him, it might look like need or greed or lust. But it is hunger, pure and simple, impure and complex. Hunger just to be *recognised* at something I once dreamt of excelling at. I want it the way I used to want sex with Matthew: hard, fast and so deep that it twanged my insides as though they were an elastic cat's cradle. I look at him hard, barely believing him after all those years, all those lies, and then I make my decision and wrench away and stride over to the sofa.

'Gran – are you ready to go to Michaela's now, love?'

'Just a minute!' She stands up, grabs her shopping bag and begins to root around in it.

'Just got to find me best teeth.'

'Gran! *Please!*'

'What?' She gapes at me, as innocent and toothless and potentially relationship-wrecking as a babe. 'Spotless, Mick's mum keeps the place. Mrs Kemp. Wants me to call 'er Veronica. "Do I 'ave to?" I said. Can't go over there in me stained teeth, see. They'd stand out like a boil on a –'

'Yes, Gran, I get your drift,' I say hastily. I can see Matthew, Mr Scum, Lord Muck or whatever he calls himself these days, leaning against the kitchen alcove wall and smirking at us. I just *know* he is contrasting, in his tiny Chinese mind, the so-called 'life' *he's* 'given' me, with all mod cons and sun-dried tomatoes, with where I've come from, which is obviously all corn plasters and commodes, as personified by Liza.

'I got these –' she extracted a pair of gnashers from her bag and jammed them in with a lack of delicacy and self-regard that made me wince '– but they got bits in –'

She pushes her face right into mine and bares her teeth. Oddly enough she looks adorable doing this, and it puts me into an even worse humour with Lord Scum, who's leaning against the wall, face in arms, stifling his sniggers by now. Better life, eh? All mod cons is about right. Hold that up against the fluorescent light of my grandmother's trusting falsies and it doesn't look such a good bargain after all.

'Perfect. Not a blemish,' I lie. To be frank, her mouth's a bit of a battlefield; it looks like the Glastonbury Festival after everyone's gone home. You expect to see one final lone ketamine merchant wandering about in there, looking for a pair of Surrey boys to unload some monumentally dodgy gear on to.

'You've been using my expensive American whitening toothpaste again, haven't you?' I twinkle.

'What biss thee after?' she asks me suspiciously, and rightly so. There's no flies on my gran. Well, there would be if I didn't keep spraying her with insect repellent. But still. She's pretty damn sharp for her age. I'll never be that sharp again; the millstone of marriage has effectively rendered me a blunt instrument, one which can still do damage to my opponent in the marital arts, but only through obdurate, brutish bashings rather than the shiv-like cunning I once prided myself on.

'I just don't want you to be late for your lovely evening out, that's all.' I pat her on the back reassuringly.

She looks around the room as though it's trying to get one over on her.

'Now.' I pull out the Ali–Liston video and pop it into her shopping bag with a sickening smirk. Don't ever let me tell you that Matthew taught me nothing. That and how to detect a lie at a distance of two continents. 'Got everything?'

'No, I tell 'ee! Me teeth . . .'

But I've got my arm unimpeachably around her now and we're moving at a rate of knots to the door. Firmly but fairly, I push her through it.

'Bye, love! Have a *wicked* time!' But of course this use of the W-word is unknown to her in its modern form, and I just glimpse her face as I close the door: puzzled, scornful and incredulous, all at once. It strikes me that a woman who's been through a lifetime of strife shouldn't be put in a position where she feels those emotions at all, singly, in the sunset of her years, let alone all at once. But hey, what do you know, it's another first for little Nicola! Give that girl a *medal*, someone! And pin it *right* through her heart!

I close the door and lean against it and I look at him. He's standing in the sunlight coming through the kitchen skylight and he looks so beautiful, like a sexy blond saint. And I get this terrible sad image in my head: of Matthew as a little boy, golden, being washed by his mother in the bathtub and him standing up and proudly and completely innocently showing off his penis, and her laughing indulgently.

And I think that if his poor mother had known on that shimmering Sixties Sunday morning what grief that precious little penis would cause in this world, she wouldn't have laughed at all. She's a woman, and she understands. So she'd have gone to the bathroom cabinet, and she'd have taken out a razorblade, and she'd have cut it off. That's what she'd have done, if she'd known.

On the CD player Ramsey Lewis celebrated 'The In Crowd' and in my bedroom I dressed up, hoping to pass as one of them.

In the doorway Matthew lounged, watching me dress; I'm not being either self-adoring or self-loathing when I say he watched me with the eye of a soft-pornographer, because that's the way Matthew looks at all women between the ages of sixteen and – I was going to say nineteen, but that's not true. Between sixteen and forty, say.

I pulled up my Wolford stockings, stepped into my Ozbek skirt and Geiger shoes, slicked on Shiseido lipstick and walked through a cloud of Femme. Of course, I did other stuff too – it wasn't a porn shoot, despite the angle of my husband's zoom. When I was finished, I knew I was beautiful.

He tried to grab me as I walked past him, but I wasn't having any. Or rather, he wasn't. Not if I had anything to do with it.

'Please don't kid yourself that I've put on my drag for your benefit, dearest; as you've so subtly pointed out, I've got a part to play and I'm going to play it. But when that door' – and I pointed at it – 'closes after the last godforsaken guest tonight, the curtain comes down. And my knickers don't come down with it.'

Eight people. Two's company, three's a crowd, four's a wife-swapping evening but eight's a boring old number and definitely a dinner party.

Me, Matt, Su and Lu, Bridget the Midget and Gav the Lav, Jonh the dyslexic and his similarly handicapped friend Sali. What a fucking shower. I dread to think what we look like an advert for as we sit around the 'space' smoking reefer and listening to jazz so wilfully obscure that each CD should come with a UN translator. Some wanky new mixed drink, probably. That or quilted toilet paper. Whatever, some jive-led junk that you've never needed and you never will. Story of my life.

They're smoking that evil crap that makes you stupid, too. Figure it. There's people all around the world spending millions of pounds on education. E-ducate: I lead out. There's people in the developed world who'd give two arms and a leg, if they had them, for a bit of book-learning to help them out of the mire they're staring at a life in. And what are we doing over here in the clever old West, pray? Spending a good part of our disposable incomes on stuff that makes us wake up one morning thinking that E equals M. C. Hammer, that's what. 'Hey?' Matthew will say whenever I make this point, 'hey, don't be laying that stuff on me when you're putting so many chemicals up your nose that I could develop my pictures just by having you sneeze on them. At least weed comes out of the *ground*,' he'll say smugly, like that completely puts the cap on it. But hey, maaan, I can think of a lot of other things that come out of the ground: hemlock, high-rises and the blood-sucking Undead. Does that mean that I should give *them* houseroom, too?

'Ewww!' Right on cue, demonstrating how stupid dope makes you – though admittedly she had a head start, and we're talking the head on a Mekon – Siobhan chokes prettily on her joint. Well, that won't be the first joint she's choked on, obviously. And what do you know, the owner of the joint which has most recently had the honour of making her gag slides across the slats like the snake-rat he is and shows her how to do it.

I watch the wet end pass from his mouth to hers, and marvel at how life sometimes seems intent solely on serving up to us as many *entendres* as we can double in a lifetime.

I jump up. 'Right. I must get the grub going.'

'But you haven't had any of this, have you, darling?' bleats Sali, pride of Tin Pan Ali, as she waves the stinking stupid-wand at me. She writes jingles and calls it creativity. Sort of like a musical version of me.

I move towards the kitchenette. 'Can't. I'm allergic.' Under my breath I mutter, hoping he'll hear, 'To my husband's slimy mouth, among other things.' But of course he only has ears for his ego, currently appearing as Bridget-Siobhan, This Year's Model.

I start to lay out the olives first, two types from Camisa, and I wonder idly why people describe people as having 'olive' skin. What do they mean – it's green, or it's black? Because neither is ever what they mean, is it? 'Olive-skinned' is shorthand for light brown, or what the racists would consider the wrong side of beige.

I start to lay out the salami and Parma ham and figs, also Soho's finest, and I think about this morning and my trip there in the pissing rain to gather this fine display for the cretinous gannets now lying around my loft. I suppose I should have felt sentimental about the alleged Good Old Days when Mr Scum and I would wander about Olde Soho hand in hand on a Sunday morning, sort of like Babes in the Wood surrounded by porn as opposed to poplars, but I couldn't. I know that other people, once the gloss has gone off a thing, feel sentimental for the old sweet days when their love was in its calf country. Frankly, though, it makes me want to throw.

People act so dumb when they're fresh in love: so clichéd, with so little imagination, and yet they think they look so cool when they're all wrapped up in each other like a Slinkee having sex with a boa constrictor. Well, when you're both thirteen and dead hard with love bites spelling out your name around your neck like an ID necklace, I suppose that's true. But the minute you're past the age of consent, in my opinion *nothing* looks naffer than hanging around doing stuff in a public space that would be better done under cover of darkness. Except when you're gay, because then it can count as rebellion.

Especially it looks pathetic when you're two metropolitan heterosexual types in your twenties or thirties. It's not rebellion then; it's just *opting in* writ large. It's 'Hey, look – I can't be as repulsive as I appear to the human eye, can I? Because *I've got a girlfriend/boyfriend*!' But the casual onlooker isn't to *know* that the person slobbering over you isn't blind as a bat, are they?

Well, I think that Sunday-morning Soho shopping is *even worse* than public mauling, when it comes to grown-up couples. And it's even more paint-by-numbers than the dismal limitations of heterosexual horizontal activity. Why *exactly* does being the three-hundredth couple that day to pick up their beans at the Algerian Coffee Store, cram a croissant at the Patisserie Valérie, browse through Italian *Vogue* at Compton News, grab a stinking hunk of *dolcelatte* at Camisa and finally doss down in front of the Soho Brasserie to spend three pigging hours tripping honest tourists up over a manky *cappuccino* make you *original*, pray? These Soho moochers, what kills me, is that they consider anyone who spends a Sunday morning ferrying the wife and two veg around Safeway to be a corporate zombie who's lost his soul. But if my relationship was so crap that I felt the need to waste anything up to four hours – half a working day – tossing about with coffee beans and Eyetie magazines rather than actually *talk* to someone, I really wouldn't be in any kind of hurry to point the finger at Mr Bridge-and-Tunnel down the garden centre. I mean I *really* wouldn't.

And then comes the day when two Filofaxes become one and spawn lots of little memos and before you can say personal organiser you too, Mr Deli-Belly, are hauling around Safeway of a Sunday *en famille*. And as your eyes rest on your wife's sour frown across a crowded boot, I bet you feel all nostalgic for those Soho Sunday mornings and think longingly of how *different* things were back then. But the thing is, they *weren't*, really. What's ended up as your Safeway nightmare had its germs in your Soho idyll, when you'd already traded your bedfest for a browse.

In the early days of your white-hot revolutionary love, when every erection feels like an act of insurrection and when every kiss is a revelation, you cram your face with takeaways and little else: sixty-nine on the living-room floor and sixty-nine on the menu, that's the perfect ratio when it comes to love. When one sixty-nine flies out of the window, though, so does the other. And then the Soho browsing starts; well, it may well smell nice and spicy, but it's still the opening steps of the dance of the death of love, no matter how you slice it.

I took the cheeky New World white from the fridge and struggled with the cork like a good little wuss. What do you know, it wouldn't budge. So I walked out intending to ask Matthew to do it. But he's already doing it. Whispering in Siobhan's ear, that is. And she's giggling and shaking her head. So we can imagine what a really filthy request *that* must be, if she's saying no.

I walk back into the kitchenette, digging the corkscrew casually into my hand. And suddenly I understand why the caged guinea pig sometimes gnaws its feet off. (I'm sure I've read somewhere that they do. Sometimes. When they're pushed.) It's to distract themselves from the greater pain of being where they know they don't belong.

Or something.

So later in the evening we're all sitting around the table, sated. And that's just after the first course. I can only imagine what the table's going to look like by the time we've finished. Or rather, I don't *have* to imagine because I've *seen* it so many times, in the homes of the people I call my friends. Talk about obscenity. I don't believe that any orgy on earth, not even one including several Germans and barnyard animals, could look worse in its satanic afterglow than the remains, both human and edible, of a middle-class dinner party for eight counting starters, desserts, fruit, wine and various chemical aperitifs and digestifs.

Only amongst the young professional middle classes can you routinely come across a dinner which is in fact *finished* and believe that it is actually only in the first stages of being *toyed* with. It's like we're all vying to put out the most lavish garbage possible, just in case the bag bursts and the Dinkies next door think we're so poor that we have to *eat* the food we buy or something. Really, why not cut out the middle man? Let's just make sure we all go shopping in Soho at the same time and throw our grub gaily into the gutter in front of each other. That way we don't have to lug it home.

But, Man being not such a logical animal, I wearily stand up and prepare to lug it all back into the kitchen. They're all drinking like the proverbial fish, in this case surely soused herrings, and this has apparently done much of the job of filling them up to the watermark, so to speak. I'm just gathering my collapsed cornucopian horn of plenty together when Gavin squeezes my hand.

'Nicole, my love-bucket, that was *it*.' He grimaces ingratiatingly. 'That's always the best way, isn't it, though – a cold smorgasbord for starters. Personally, I *hate* it when people go to any trouble – it's so *eighties*.'

Well, if I hadn't gone to any trouble cooking the damn stuff, I was sure making up for lost time now as I juggled eight plates and the best part of an uneaten feast for a family of Mormons. God *forbid* that anybody should lift a finger, of course. I smiled determinedly. 'Thanks, Gavin.'

'Please, Nic. Call me Gav.' As I stare at him, trying to work out whether he is trying to imitate Roger Moore as James Bond or Pee Wee Herman as Oscar Wilde, I distinctly felt the sexually perplexed pondlife run his hand up my leg and under my skirt. I was amazed, and I can't believe my gaze didn't say so. But no. Our eyes locked. He smiled. He had an emerald in one front tooth. 'Rhymes with "have" . . .'

I gape at him. 'Right. Cheers. Gav.' I could hear my voice rising, like some prim Western miss alarmed by Calamity Jane's buckskins. 'Matt, can you come and help me for a tick? Please, babes?'

He pulls away from Siobhan, sort of like a man peeling off a used condom, and gets drunkenly to his feet. 'You got it, angel.'

'He's a New Man!' Siobhan shrieks. Though in her book this is probably a man who actually *stops* the car before demanding a blow job.

I'm not exactly the last of the Mohicans, but my ears

are plenty keen enough to hear Sali smirk, 'But *darling*, I thought *old* men were your speciality . . .'

There is nowhere to go but the toilet. I mean it this time, I've had it with this loft-living shtick. I grab him by the shirtfront and pull him in and lock the door.

He leers grotesquely at me, the clueless sot. 'Right now, baby? OK. But say pleeeze . . .'

'Shut up!' I hiss. 'That *Gavin*! Did you *see* him?'

'What?'

'He was mauling me! Right there at the table!'

'Was he?'

'I thought he was gay! You *said* he was!'

He considers this. 'Well, he was. But a lot of gay guys are rediscovering the straight side of their sexuality these days. I guess Gav's one of them.'

'Well, tell him to go and discover it with somebody else.' I can't believe how calmly he's taking this. 'Because, quite frankly, I've been involved in enough discovery, adventure and experimentation of the interpersonal variety to last me nine bloody lifetimes! And let me tell you – and you can tell "Gav" – that a complete absence of all known stimuli is what I'm dreaming of right now! Especially in the carnal knowledge Trivial Pursuit department.'

He sneers at me, trying to be cool and going cross-eyed instead. 'You're really pretty uptight, aren't you, babes?'

'No, I'm not, actually.' My head seems to clear suddenly and I lean against the toilet door, despising him from what feels like a great height. I am vertiginous with virtue. 'I'm really pretty damn relaxed. Especially when *you're* not here. And I happen to think that it's just a little uptight to have to go around proving you can still *do it* every day of the year. As though your cock might drop off if you don't use it ceaselessly. That's a bit sad, isn't it? Aren't you boys *ever* going to stop playing with yourselves? Aren't you ever going to grow up?'

I can see him groping for the perfect put-down. Let's face it, stone-cold sober he's hardly a candidate for *Call My Bluff*. Drunk, he can just about tell his left from his right, but not if he's been looking in a mirror recently. Finally, his lips curl like Elvis asked to French-kiss the Coasters and he slurs: 'Sorry, *Mum*.'

He closed the door quietly behind him. For some reason that always gets to me. Quiet as the grave of love. I stared into the toilet and my vision swam. I really thought for a moment that I could see my marriage certificate bobbing there beneath the beatific blue water.

'My marriage,' I said softly, peering. 'My marriage is down the toilet!'

The water seemed to shimmer as if in agreement. Great! Now even the john was patronising me.

I stood up straight, suddenly pushed beyond endurance. I felt like my gran when my mum made that infamous jelly in the po. I wrenched off my wedding ring and I threw it literally into the blue. The marriage certificate shivered and shattered and the ring went straight down the chute.

I opened the door and stepped out into the frowsy fog of stoned, drunken chatter. I went straight to the oven and, careful not to burn my fingers, removed the casserole. I set it down and stirred it.

As if I had willed it so, Liza's very best teeth surfaced, yellow and hot and primitive as bones. Had I put them there, or had she? Whatever, I just had to laugh.

I carried the casserole to the table in my oven gloves, very serving-wench. I could feel Gav the Hav appraising me. I stood there and smiled at their upturned faces. For a moment, for what they were about to receive, I almost loved them.

I served Sali, then Jonh, then Su, then Lu. Finally only my favourites were left. I looked from Gavin, to Siobhan, to my darling love, and time seemed suspended, suspended in a thick dark soup.

'Eeny, meeny, miney –' and my ladle of destiny struck.

I served them up sideways, garnished them with a sprig of thyme and gave the plate to Gavin with a flourish that wouldn't have disgraced a principal boy. I was pleased to see that he looked completely horrified in the split second before I leant across the table, put my face *right* up against his and shouted, for all the world as though it was *boo*!: 'MO!'

Chapter **Fourteen**

Well, you can create your own pizza from here on in. A good, solid base of screeching all round and back for seconds with a double helping of accusations and counter-accusations, alternated neatly like circles of pepperoni and green pepper. Add something fishy – Siobhan or an anchovy – and take it away. As she has my husband. So here I stand, at last, where I knew I always would be one day. Alone.

I walk around the loft, shell-shocked, yet even now trying to do constructive stuff – drink the remnants from glasses, smoke the longer butts – like the good, mad housewife I am. Finally I find that there's no compulsive cleaning left to be done – the glasses are empty and the butts are smoked – so I do what comes naturally. I sit on the floor, hug my knees, hum softly, and sob.

I don't know how long I'm like this, but I bet I could get some sort of school certificate just for showing up all that time, if I thought to ask. But just before I do, I hear the sound of a key in the lock.

I stand up, ready to tell him exactly where to go. Which is right on to the bed, where I'll make servile, sluttish love to him for as long as it takes. Well, for seven minutes or so. Which even *that* he doesn't deserve, strictly speaking.

Only of course it isn't him. It is Liza and her demon spawn – Michaela Kemp, I believe it calls itself. It's toting a small suitcase. And in it, I imagine, she carries what is left of my heart and my soul.

I scramble to my feet. 'Gran! He's left me!'

'Yeah. We 'eard.'

Liza moves in slo-mo to the bureau by the bed and Michaela floats after her, or so it seems. Liza opens a drawer and points to it. Michaela opens the suitcase.

'Well, *she's* not moving in!' I shout.

Michaela turns to me and smiles as if all her Christmases have come at once and she's getting sex toys for all of them. 'No. *Nan's* moving out. *She's* the cat's mother.'

I look at Gran, and she looks away. I can't believe that this could happen. Anything else. I believed that I could grow up to be a raging mediocrity at the only thing I'd ever wanted to do, and what do you know? I was. I believed that my husband could leave me and, hey, he more than lived up to my expectations. I believed that one day I would reach a place in my life when I would wake up each morning and look at what I had with the purest of dismays, and, knock me down with a feather, I do. But I never believed for a minute that my gran would turn away from me.

But she's nodding, nodding as she supervises Michaela's packing. 'Veronica, Mrs Kemp, she 'eard the argufying. Said as 'ow I shouldn't 'ave to put up with it at my age. She'm right, too. I'll 'ave a proper bedroom at Mick's place. And me own telly. You name it . . .'

'*And* a budgie,' gloats Demon Spawn. 'Lux the Second . . .'

I stagger towards her, I literally stagger because I feel I've been shot. 'But Gran . . .' I grab her in a botched hug and I can feel all her bones and smell her in all her mildewed glory. 'You can't leave me! You can't! I'm only little!'

She pushes me away, and when I look at her face there is a look of what I can only describe as . . . yes, it is real *distaste*. I want to cry.

And then I hear the Thing laughing.

Liza turns to her and points at the door. 'You. Mick. 'Op it.'

The brat pouts, its sport for the night ruined. 'But Mum said –'

'Thy mum bisn't my mum. Thee do as I say.'

Michaela stands glaring at me, then slams out. As she gets into the lift, I can hear her whistling 'I'm 'Enery the Eighth, I Am'. It seems so wretchedly appropriate: a soulless America-fed Cockney brat singing a song which was a soulless parody of Cockney in the first place and which she'd probably never even heard until she saw *Ghost*. Come and get your culture, England! God help us.

Liza holds her arms out to me, but I know she doesn't mean it. 'Sit down, my wench. Come on, sit thee down. And stop creating.'

She goes to the sofa and sits down and I sit beside her and bury my face in her shoulder. It's true, Matthew was right, she *does* smell awful. I never want to breathe anything else.

'Please. Gran! Please don't go! Don't leave me!'

'I'll only be across the road,' she points out – reasonably, I must admit – while patting my back. 'Thee can wave to me. When thee's not too busy. When the scribbling stops. I can come over and visit thee every day. Do yer shopping for 'ee.' She laughs. 'Like you used to for me, when you was meant to be at school.'

'Oh, Gran,' I wail. 'I so wanted it to be the way it was in the old days!'

She thinks about this. I sit back and look at her face and I can see that she really is thinking for once. 'It can be,' she says slowly, 'it can be. But only a bit. You can 'ave things a bit the way they were. But if you tries for the 'ole thing, it disappears altogether. Just a bit is the best way.'

'Those were great days, weren't they?' I blub. 'When I was young?'

Liza smiles. 'They were great days for me. All my grandchirren round me. All your parents, runnin' round after the lot of you! As good as *The Keystone Cops*, it was. I used to sit there when they came looking for thee, and thee'd be 'iding under the bed, and I'd look at all your parents and think, Thees may be bringin' in the money these days, an' I may be old and ignorant. But I'm still the boss! 'Cos I got your *children*! They'm *mine*!' She laughs, then frowns. 'But think back, Nic'la. *You* dissn't like it all that much – remember? You used to make yerself sick sometimes so you wouldn't 'ave to go to school. All thee wanted to do was scribble and run away to London. Thee was a whiney little wench then – like thee's a whiney little wench now. And I loved thee then, as I love thee now.'

She laughs again. 'But I was bleeding glad when thee finally 'opped it to London, I can tell thee!' She holds my face in her hands and squints at me. 'Thee's got what thee wanted. So what's yer problem?'

'My marriage . . .' I trail off weakly, not really knowing what I want to say.

She chuckles like the fiend in need she truly is: 'From what I 'eard, thee 'asn't got a marriage no more. But thee should be glad of that, too, from what I've seen of that specimen. Wish we'd 'ad divorce in my day – I could 'ave 'ad it sweet.' She ruffles my hair. 'But then I'd never have had you. My Nicky.'

That turned on the taps, natch. 'Oh, Gran!'

So she strokes my hair and speaks philosophically. 'See, that's the great thing about our family. If we'd 'av been Roman Candles, you'd be lumbered. But the Sharp women 'ave always been prostitutes – like you. Divorce 'im. No problemo – Mick says that.'

'Oh, Gran!'

How many times have I said these words over the past few months? A few hundred times too many, I think. Because they're words of one syllable, aren't they? Which has been all my poor battered brain has been up to. Marriage makes children of most of us, all but the lucky few, and bad marriages make abused children of us; just like parents, we allow our partners to yell at us, hit us and generally treat us with a level of discourtesy and brutality which they would never *dream* of doling out to the stranger – the *perfect* stranger, so unlike the fallible lovefool at home – in the street.

You know how lying in bed too long is meant to waste your muscles? Well, lying in marriage too long wastes your brain. Wasted on the in and out, the cut and thrust of marital combat. Well, I've had enough. A mind is a terrible thing to waste, and I've spent too long on the road to nowhere, positively revelling in my powerlessness, like someone on a white-knuckle ride. We spend so much time as children wanting only to be tall enough to go on the scary rides that when we finally get the chance to we'd rather die than say we were wrong, and can we have our money back and *can I go home, can I go home?* But of course that's all we want by then. When we realise that marriage is the white-knuckle ride. The white-knuckle, black-eye, red-mist ride that we're all too scared to scream out and get off. Because if we do the grown-ups will smirk and snigger and put us to bed with a bowl of Heinz Big Soup. Because we weren't big enough after all.

That's what marriage is, for most women, for women who had the good fortune to grow up cherished by their parents: exchanging a happy family for a hellish one. Exchanging a father, a man who despite the blinkers of his upbringing had come, painfully and triumphantly, to accept this swirling, sassy maelstrom whom he once called his little girl as *real*, as capable and as culpable as all his sons, for a husband who hasn't learnt anything about women *at all* because he thought he knew everything already. I'll tell you a thing, and it's a *terrible* thing. I know for sure that my generation of women fake orgasms with men *so much more* than our mothers did. Fake everything. Love, laughter, happy ever after.

Women today. It kills me. We all know, and none of us admit it. Except screaming dykes, and I wouldn't want the number of *their* manicurist.

So much ourselves, at last; at work with our colleagues, at rest with our friends, at play with our children. So much revealed and, when revealed, accomplished. And then, like larceny, like loathsomeness, this *other* thing, with men. This soft, slimy, slothful slug. This grimacing geisha. And why? Just tell me, *why*? It's not even fun any more. Hell – it's not even fun for *them* any more. We all want to end it now. Put it out of its misery. Marriage: it's not all that's wrong with the world. But right here, right now, for healthy adult women during the closing steps of the twentieth century, it's most of what's wrong. Yoked together, male and female, on the hamster wheel of their own surrender to the system, and each hating the other for being the blood witness of their own compromise and shame.

So that's why I say 'Oh, Gran!' the way I do; laughing, not drowning. Because at last I realise that I'm well out of it. At last, I am free.

And for once, *just this once* – and I'll kill you if you ever mention it again – that nasty little Cockney-sucker would appear to be right. There really is, to use the vernacular, no problemo. Why couldn't I see that before?

When Gran had gone, promising to come back at nine the next morning to watch the early-morning WWF, I stood and looked around my loft. It needed loving, and I was the girl for the job.

I whirled through it like a white tornado, with squeegees for feet and dusters for hands, until every surface was clean enough to sniff the purest Peruvian off.

And then I was in a very deep bubble bath, smelling of vanilla, which smells of pride, and of comfort, and of joy.

And I was in a long, thick, towelling dressing gown, which feels like all the protection men ever promised you in pursuit of the perfect suck job.

And then I was making myself Butterscotch Instant Whip and hot Ribena, which together tastes as swirling and sweet and one hundred per cent supportive as true love is supposed to be.

And then I selected a book from my precious cache – *Ballet Shoes*. And as I lay down on the bed with it, I knew that in the self-contained struggles of the Fossil sisters I would find far more soul, sass and succour than in the sympathetic phone calls of my friends. Because the Fossil sisters were *girls*, small and mobile and inviolate units, while my friends are *women*, defined by *men*, and they cannot see perfect aloneness as anything more than the absence of a man.

I put on a video and hit the PAUSE button – *The Singing Ringing Tree*. Because life is as strange and outrageous as this, and as hard to understand sometimes. But if you make the effort, it's worth it.

I looked around the loft, which had previously seemed to me to be the tomb of my love, and I saw it for what it was: a beautiful, pristine playpen in which I was free to be myself without any parent, or parent substitute who just happened to be shagging me, pushing me around.

And so I said softly to myself, 'I'm alone.' Almost wonderingly.

And then I shouted – louder than I've ever shouted in sorrow or anger – 'I'M ALONE!'

And I fell on to the bed, pressed the PLAY button, grabbed my Instant Whip and felt my life begin to unwind.